"Oh, Nina!" Lucas said softly, touching a tear with his fingertip. "What's wrong?"

Nina sucked in her breath, and before she could say "Nothing," Lucas had his arms around her. His embrace engulfed her. Nina pressed her tiny round face into his chest.

"I'm getting your sweatshirt all wet," she said.

"It's okay," Lucas said, rubbing her back. "It's all right. Everything's going to be all right."

Nina didn't want to feel this way.

But she *needed* to. She needed to feel that someone cared for her. But why did it have to be Lucas?

Don't miss any of the books in
Making Out
by Katherine Applegate
from Avon Books

Coming Soon

MAKING OUT #23

Lara gets lucky

KATHERINE APPLEGATE

AVON BOOKS

An Imprint of HarperCollins Publishers

Library of Congress Catalog Card Number: 99-95488
ISBN: 0-380-81527-3

First Avon edition, 2000

AVON TRADEMARK REG. U.S. PAT. OFF. AND IN OTHER COUNTRIES,
MARCA REGISTRADA, HECHO EN U.S.A.

Zoey

How happy am I to be home from my heinous internship in Washington, D.C.? Let me count the ways.

1. <u>Sleeping</u> <u>in</u> my ~~bed~~. What a relief. The one hundred percent cotton blue-and-white-striped oxford cloth sheets that smell like laundry detergent and fabric softener. The plaid blankets special-ordered from L.L. Bean. The down-filled pillows. To think I'd almost gotten used to the overstarched excuses for linens they had in the youth hostel.

2. <u>Home-cooked</u> <u>food</u>. Some people, my best friend Nina, to name one, would think it was the coup of

the century to be able to eat fast food morning, noon, and night, which is what I ended up doing in D.C. (I'm sorry, but those hostel offerings were less than inedible.) But I myself couldn't be more happy to be dining on clam chowder. Even last night's party was perfect culinarywise, though it was potluck. Come to think of it, the party would have been perfect everythingwise were it not for two things: My annoying half sister, Lara, showed up, and my boyfriend and I didn't get to spend much quality time together. (Which brings me to #3 on the list.)

3. <u>Lucas.</u> I know, I know, it's not like I've been gone for that long,

but I really missed him. I love cupping his face in my hands while curling strands of his blond hair around my index fingers as I give him quick kisses on his forever-sun-chapped lips. Of course, we didn't get in too much fooling-around time last night—what with all of my family and friends being there. (Which, of course, brings me to #4.)

4. <u>Nina.</u> Spending the last few days with my roommate from hell, aka Miss Perky Teen America, aka MaryBeth, really made me appreciate Nina and all her adorable quirks. Mary-Beth's quirks were very unadorable. More like deplorable. So what if Nina hates to leave her bedroom? So what if she's taken to

wearing black corduroys and T-shirts with inscrutable sayings on them on a daily basis? At least she's always interesting. And anyway, I always have my other best friend, Aisha, if I need to counter Nina's opinions with ones that are somewhat more rational. (Incidentally, where was Aisha last night? I'll have to call her later today.)

This list could go on forever. Suffice it to say, I'm really happy to be home and no longer in Washington, D.C. Do I sound like an ingrate? I hope not. It's not that I wasn't totally honored to be included in a conference for promising young journalists held in our nation's capital. It's

just that, well, it came at a
really bad time.

I mean, Lucas's father
just died. He tried to act
tough when I told him I
was supposed to go to the
conference right after the
funeral; in fact, he even
encouraged me to go, saying
he had a lot of work to do
on his dad's fishing boat
and everything. But I know
him too well. Besides, what
good is having a girlfriend
if she's not there when
you need her? I know
Nina's been looking out
for him, but it's not like
they're close friends.
Anyway, she's not exactly
in the best of shape
herself, considering that
she and my brother, Ben-
jamin, just broke up.
(Mental note: Get on Ben-
jamin's case for making

the stupidest mistake of
his life.)

Looking back on it, I
realize now that I
shouldn't have gone to
D.C. I should never have
abandoned Lucas. Not right
now, not when he needs
me. A parent's death can't
be easy, especially for someone like Lucas, who has
the tendency to hold back,
keep things in. (I'm sorry
to lapse into psychobabble,
but I think I know
Lucas pretty well after
everything we've been
through together.) It was a
long time ago, but I still
remember when Nina and
Claire's mom died. Nina
was, well, unhappy doesn't
begin to cover it. I wish
that Lucas and Nina were
better friends. She might be
able to help him.

Now that I'm back, I'll make it a point that Lucas and Nina spend time together. The three of us can hang out. And maybe when Benjamin comes to his senses, it can be the four of us.

There's not much time left until I go away to college. I've got to use this time to show Lucas how much I love him and appreciate him. I'm never going to let Lucas down again.

Nina

For some reason I remember my junior-high-school bathroom vividly. There were hearts drawn on the walls in thick black indelible marker that said things like Brian and Belinda 2Gether 4Ever. Well, I think that those had a bad effect on my brain or something because I've always believed that love meant forever.

Pretty dumb, huh?

Maybe I sound like a relic from one of those old girl-meets-boy-marries-girl-and-they-live-happily-ever-after movies that I watch on cable when nothing else is on, but I always thought that was kind of how it worked. Or at least that was how it would work for me.

It took me a long time to convince Benjamin Passmore that he and I should be together. And then it was over. He ended it. Just like that.

You know that song they play on the old fogy's radio station, "Breaking Up Is Hard to Do"? Boy, do those cheeseheads not know what they're talking about. Breaking up is easy to do; at least it was for Benjamin.

At first after Benjamin and I broke up, I felt this incredible ache. And I don't just mean in my heart. I mean all over. In my arms and my legs, in every finger and every toe, in the back of my throat and the pit of my stomach (though that might be the sour cream and onion potato chips I've gotten addicted to).

The only time the ache has gone away involved kissing Lucas Cabral.

When I kissed Lucas, not only did the ache dissolve, it was replaced with a tingly feeling, like the kind you feel when the dentist cleans your gums, only all over, and it felt good. Really good.

But when it was over, the ache came back.

It's okay. The ache doesn't really bother me anymore. I go to sleep with it and wake up with it. I walk aimlessly around the island with it.

And since the only cure for it seems to involve kissing my best friend's boyfriend, I guess I better get used to it.

One

Zoey's hands and arms were submerged in dirty dish-water.

This wasn't exactly how she'd planned to spend her first morning back on Chatham Island—scraping the remains of lobster fricassee off china plates and scrubbing the soup tureen until it was free of congealed clam chowder. But she'd woken up at five A.M., an hour to which she was totally unaccustomed, and although she'd tried to go back to sleep, for some reason that had proved impossible. Instead she'd lain in bed for a while, snuggling under the blankets, writing in her journal and letting her mind drift. In the end she'd had too much energy to stay still.

Now it was 6:45 A.M., and Zoey had already taken a jog along Leeward Drive, showered, dressed, and unpacked the suitcases she'd taken with her to the journalism conference in Washington, D.C. She'd divided her dirty clothes into "to be washed in the machine" and "to be washed by hand" and deposited a jumble of jeans, sweatshirts, and underthings in the washing machine out in the garage. She listened now for the whooshing sound that meant the rinse cycle was ending and the spin cycle was beginning. That would mean three minutes until it was time to move the load to the dryer.

Zoey had gone to the kitchen to have a glass of orange juice and a bowl of cornflakes and found herself confronted with a massive pile of pots, pans, dishes, and silverware. Her first instinct was to run away and pretend she had never seen this disaster area, but then she'd thought better of herself. After all, the mess was a result of the party from the night before, a party in honor of her homecoming.

The party had been really good, just as good as the high-school graduation party she and Benjamin had thrown at the beginning of the summer. Actually, Zoey considered, last night's party was better than the graduation party. Because Lucas was there.

Zoey pushed her hands deeper into the sudsy water in order to pull the stopper out of the drain. The pipes made a gurgling sound as the water began to drain. Zoey stared at her wet hands. They were red from the hot water, and the tips of her fingers were wrinkled like raisins. They reminded her of Lucas's hands when he got off the fishing boat, pinched from the salty sea water and sunburned.

Lucas has already gone to work, Zoey thought, sighing. It really was too bad that Lucas had to work on his dad's fishing boat. As the daughter of restaurant owners, Zoey knew all about family obligations. *Don't even compare an occasional dinner shift at the plush family restaurant to what Lucas has to do,* Zoey scolded herself. If only Lucas didn't see working on the boat as such a stigma, Zoey thought. If only he could see that it'd be over soon. That he'd be off to college soon. Not that he was too excited about the University of Maine, either.

Zoey knew she had to make every second remaining in the summer count. Zoey smiled as she contemplated the many ways she'd shower Lucas with affection. They'd make out in the dark movie theater at the mall in Weymouth, take long walks along the beach, hang out in the family room downstairs, watching music videos. *I won't even make him change the channel for MTV TRL,* Zoey thought, smiling to herself.

"You look like quite the happy homemaker."

Zoey whipped around to see her brother, Benjamin, standing in the middle of the kitchen, grinning. He was dressed in a black wet suit with royal blue stripes down the side. His nose was covered with a white splotch of zinc oxide. His wet hair was held back by a pair of blue plastic sunglasses that were strategically placed on the top of his head. Zoey couldn't help but think back to the time when Benjamin's sunglasses weren't just a fashion accessory. In fact, sometimes she still expected her once blind brother to be wearing his trademark black Ray-Ban sunglasses and a cynical smirk. Not that she missed the trappings of Benjamin's blindness; it was just that, well, somehow this happy-go-lucky, sporty Benjamin wasn't the same person.

"It's about time someone in this house got up," Zoey said, walking over to her brother and flipping some soapsuds in his general direction.

"The Passmores aren't known for their early bird habits," Benjamin replied as he crossed the kitchen and opened the refrigerator.

Zoey nodded. "I could make you a smoothie if you want," she offered.

"Hmmm . . . sounds . . . healthy," Benjamin answered, as if healthy food was a concept he was unfamiliar with. He grabbed a bottle of water from the refrigerator, shut it, and took a seat at the kitchen table. "Hey, not that I mind the company, but why are you up so early?" Benjamin paused. "Is it because you're planning on catching some waves with me?"

"Not quite," Zoey answered, peeling a banana and throwing it in the blender. "I just couldn't sleep."

"Why not?" Benjamin asked.

The ice clattered as Zoey dropped it in with the banana. "I guess I'm just excited to be home."

"I see," Benjamin replied. "Well, since you are up, you could come with me. Surfing is good for the soul, you know."

Zoey looked at him. *But it can be dangerous,* she wanted to say to Benjamin, but she didn't.

Zoey had to wonder if Benjamin could read her mind because he immediately responded with: "You know, you could be happy that I'm getting out of the house and taking in the outdoors. You'd think people around here want me to be blind again or something."

Zoey poured some orange juice in the blender and pressed mix. "Benjamin, don't even joke about that," she said over the whirring noise. "It's just that—"

"It's just that what?" Benjamin asked. Zoey could hear the defensiveness in his voice.

"It's just that nothing," Zoey responded curtly. "I just worry about you, that's all."

"There's nothing to worry about," Benjamin answered. Zoey could hear his tone softening. He knew she really cared, even if he wanted to be independent.

"Well, I just don't want you to take too many risks too fast," she answered.

"Live for the present is how I see it," Benjamin replied.

Zoey turned off the blender and poured the orangy mush into a large blue plastic glass. She wanted to press the topic, but she had to keep in mind that Benjamin was still incredibly sensitive about his sight. She decided to leave him alone. "Maybe Nina and I will come by the beach later," she added brightly.

"Zo," Benjamin said between gulps of smoothie, "is that what this is about? Me and Nina? Look, we've grown apart. There's no point in kidding ourselves. Nina and I are very different people."

15

"Right," Zoey replied disbelievingly. No matter what her brother said, she didn't believe him. He and Nina were meant to be together. Just like Zoey and Lucas were meant to be together.

"Well, as much as I'd like to continue this conversation, I gotta go. I'm meeting some buddies at the beach," Benjamin said abruptly, standing up. He placed the empty glass in the sink. "Thanks for breakfast, Zo."

"Be careful, Benjamin," Zoey called out.

"Hey!" Benjamin answered back. "Have a little faith!" Zoey heard the front door slam behind him. She watched from the kitchen window as Benjamin hurried down the front walk, his surfboard under his arm.

Zoey rinsed Benjamin's glass and looked at the clock above the window. Seven-fifteen A.M. Lucas should be back from his first work shift now. He sometimes came back home for an hour after the morning shift. *Maybe he's eating breakfast now,* she thought. It could be the perfect time to go visit.

Zoey ran upstairs to brush her hair and put some moisturizer on her face, maybe even a little lip gloss. Her heart beat quickly as she thought about surprising Lucas with a morning call. As she switched on the bathroom light, she remembered that her laundry was probably ready to be dried. *I'll get to it later,* she decided. *Now Lucas needs me.*

Claire stared at the blank wall.

She'd been staring at the blank wall for a good two hours now. Or was it three hours? At some point during the long, miserable, and sleepless night, Claire had lost count.

The venetian blinds on the window created barlike shadows on the wall. *How fitting,* she thought. Claire felt like a prisoner.

It wasn't like Claire couldn't leave her bedroom if she

16

wanted to; she could. In fact, Claire wanted nothing more than to trudge down to the kitchen in her slippers and drink a glass of orange juice freshly squeezed by the Geigers' housekeeper, Janelle. Then again, Claire wanted nothing less than to be confronted by her father and his litany of morning niceties. "Good morning, Claire!" he'd trumpet, the business section of the local newspaper in one hand, a cup of vitamin-C-enriched herbal tea in the other. (His new wife, Sarah Mendel, had squelched his A.M. two-cup-of-coffee habit upon moving in. "His heart can't take it!" she'd gasped.) "And how did you sleep last night, Claire?" he'd ask, ever courteous.

Claire couldn't imagine how she'd answer that. "Well, Dad, let's see, from eleven P.M. to two A.M. my sleep was derailed by involuntary trembling that overtook my body, at two-thirty A.M. the dry heaving started, and some point soon after I was overcome with paranoid delusions. . . . So, you know, about par for the course, lately."

No, Claire didn't see that happening. Because if she told her father that, he'd ask her what she was troubled about, and then she'd have to break it to him. "Don't freak out, Dad," she'd have to say. "But I'm being stalked by a madman."

"I'm being stalked." Claire mumbled the words to herself. It wasn't like she needed to say the words to believe them. All she had to do was look toward the tattered clothes that filled her closet to be reminded of yesterday evening's real-life nightmare.

Claire had returned from Zoey Passmore's party at about eleven P.M. As far as she was concerned, the party had been decent, nothing more. She'd had a good time talking to Benjamin and the crab fritters had been pretty tasty, but other than that, she'd been bored. Well, maybe bored wasn't the right word. The truth was that Claire might have had a good time if she hadn't been fidgety and distracted. Throughout the party Claire was haunted by the nagging feeling that the stalker was out there, waiting for her. He'd had her so on edge that every time she'd gone to the bathroom, she'd checked behind the shower curtain to make sure nobody was there. It was a lucky thing nobody had been there. She'd checked by stabbing the shower curtain with her daggerlike stiletto heel.

As it turned out, Claire had nothing to worry about. The stalker hadn't been watching her every move at the Passmores' party. Instead he'd been over at her house. He'd somehow managed to get in—perhaps through the window, perhaps through the back door, Claire wasn't sure. He'd gotten into her room, emptied the contents of her dresser, removed all the clothes, and slashed them. Then he'd moved on to her closet. He'd left nothing intact. Hanging off the wooden hangers in Claire's closet were frayed ribbons that once were dresses; crumpled in her drawers were sliced-up nightgowns, torn T-shirts, and strips of denim that used to be jeans.

The stalker had been at it for a few weeks now, but this was the farthest he'd gone. There'd been phone calls, nasty notes, and an unnerving nude photo of her. (Much to the chagrin of her family members, Claire had gone so far as to have their number changed.)

Ever since it started happening, Claire had been trying to think methodically about it all, tried to scour her mind for someone who felt vengeful toward her. Unfortunately she didn't have to scour very hard. In fact, Claire wondered briefly whether there might be an entire club of people out to get her. A support group, as it were. They could have T-shirts with I Love to Scare Claire on the front.

At one particularly nightmarish moment during Claire's fitful night she'd concluded that the shredding had to be an inside job. Who else could have gotten in and out of the house in such a short time?

Was it Sarah Mendel? She certainly had the motive. After all, she hated the fact that Claire was dating her son, Aaron. She was always saying it was "unhealthy," considering that she was married to Claire's father. Secretly Claire suspected that Mama Mendel didn't think Claire was good enough for her precious son. Or maybe she was seeking vengeance for Claire's prewedding misdemeanors—when she'd schemed and plotted to break up her father and Sarah's coming marriage. It was conceivable that Sarah held a grudge.

Was it Nina, Claire's irascible and unpredictable sister? For as long as Claire could remember, her relationship with her younger sister, Nina, had been strained. But so strained that Nina would take to stalking her? Claire didn't think so. Stalking took a lot of premeditation, a lot of energy; Nina was too lazy. Plus she'd been at the Passmores' house when the slashing had occurred.

So maybe it was Janelle. Claire wasn't always as polite to Janelle as she should be. Maybe she'd finally pushed Janelle too far? It seemed unlikely that Janelle would have destroyed clothes, though. After all, she was the one who'd washed and ironed them all. Claire couldn't imagine Janelle ever being so wasteful. Claire vividly remembered the time that Nina had cut off the top of her gray Weymouth High School sweatshirt. (She had been doing the eighties *Flashdance* look for Halloween.) Janelle had gone positively batty on her.

The only insider left was her dad. But what motive could he possibly have? Temporary insanity as a result of caffeine withdrawal?

Claire knew that she was being absurd, but she was at her wits' end. Of course nobody in her house was trying to get her. But somebody was.

Aisha

<u>Lies</u>

I know a lot about lies. And not because I've told a lot of them. Well, okay, okay, there was that major debacle at the senior prom when I didn't tell my boyfriend, Christopher, that I'd consented to go with someone else. That was somewhat sleazy.

I know a lot about lies because a lot of them have been told to me; nearly an infinite number, in fact.

And I would like to thank Christopher Shupe for that. He's the man I thought I was going to spend the rest of my life with, the man I thought I was going to be able to trust, confide in, and everything else.

Christopher Shupe was the one thing I thought I could count on. And now look. Here I am about to go away to college in

Princeton, New Jersey. I'm trying to get my life in order, and here he goes and shakes everything up.

I think about the lies he told me. I count them, add them up, try to make any logical sense of them that I can. (I'm a scientist, after all, and if it doesn't make logical sense, well, then, I'm not really interested.)

Here's what I know: Christopher was married before. To a pretty girl named Carina Connelly. She was a drug addict. It was a short marriage. They got it annulled. Christopher moved to Chatham Island. The end.

I got all this information from Kendra, Christopher's sister. (Mind you, that was another lie he told me. The guy is so secretive, it took him a million years to divulge to me that the girl living in his house was actually his sister.)

Anyway, that's as much of the truth as I know I've asked Christopher to tell me everything. Instead he's told me nothing

Nina

<u>Lies</u>

Lies get such a bad rap. If you ask me, sometimes they can be a good thing.

Like say for instance you'd kissed your best friend's boyfriend. Of course, this is a hypothetical scenario and has nothing to do with me. But let's consider it, anyway. What if your best friend noticed you were acting weird and asked you what was up?

Would you tell it like it is? Would you say, "Well — I'm acting like a freak because I made out with the guy who claims he loves only you. And I really liked it."

No, I don't think you'd say that at all. I think you'd lie. I think you'd say, "I don't know what you're talking about. I'm only acting a little weird because I'm still in love with my old boyfriend who just happens to be your brother; it's absolutely not because I think I might be falling in love with your boyfriend."

I think you'd say that.

Even if it wasn't true.

Especially if it wasn't.

Two

Benjamin marveled at the expanse of white and blue before him. All that sand. All that water. To think that once upon a time—not long ago, in fact—it had all been darkness.

"Hey, dude," a guy called out.

"S'up, dude!" another guy cried out.

"Surf's up, that's what!" another one responded before Benjamin could say anything.

Benjamin smiled. Zoey just didn't get it. Neither did Nina, for that matter.

The way Benjamin saw it, there was something almost poetic about surfing. The slapping sound of the surfboard hitting the water, the crackling sound of the waves when you were paddling out into the vastness, the buzzing sound of the board as you ripped along the crest of a big one.

All of it sounded as good to Benjamin as the classical music he used to listen to when he was blind. Benjamin thought back to his past life for a moment: long days spent in his bedroom, the speakers blaring with the maudlin strains of Stravinsky as he wore sunglasses in the dark. He thought about how he had to rely on other people to read to him, to do things for him. He dug his feet into the sand and exhaled deeply, letting the beach air fill his lungs. Thank God those days were behind him.

Benjamin's reminiscences were interrupted. "What's up, Beno? Glad you made it out to Weymouth!"

Addled, Benjamin turned to see Bob, one of his surfer buddies, standing next to him. "Thanks, dude," Benjamin answered. "What's up with you?"

"Cool, man," Bob answered. "Hey, you got to get those sunglasses checked out or something."

"Huh?" Benjamin replied, confused.

"I just ran up from the shore, man. I was waving to you from down there, but I guess you couldn't see me or something. You just missed a massive ride, man. It was awesome."

"Oh, uh, I guess I didn't see you," Benjamin replied. "I guess these glasses are scratched."

"They're not the only thing that's scratched," Bob said.

"What do you mean?" Benjamin asked. He'd mastered a lot of surfing lingo, but sometimes Bob lost him with a new one.

"I mean your board, dude," Bob replied, laughing. "Check out those scratches."

Benjamin looked at the board. He squinted hard. Scratches. He didn't see any scratches.

"Look at 'em, man; they're huge. Scratches like that can really harsh your ride," Bob was saying.

Benjamin rubbed his hands against the board. Bob was right. The board's smooth surface was covered with tiny rough lines. "Um, I guess I didn't notice," Benjamin stammered.

"Well, it's nothing a little wax can't help," Bob answered. "I think I got some in my bag. But you ought to be careful out there today. We'll wax it up, but you still might need to take it to the shop."

Benjamin nodded and followed Bob down toward

the shore. "I really appreciate your help, dude," he said.

"What's a little wax between buds?" Bob replied, laughing again. "Still, though, you gotta make sure you're always checking your board, dude. You gotta give it a good once-over before you ride, you know. Just to be safe."

Benjamin nodded again. *It's nothing,* he said to himself. *This isn't a problem. I just didn't see the scratches because of the sun. It's really sunny out today. Brutal.*

"Here's my stuff," Bob said, pointing to a towel he'd set up near the lifeguard chair. "Park it."

"Don't mind if I do," Benjamin replied, taking a seat in the sand and watching Bob as he dipped his hand into his knapsack and pulled out a yellow tub of surfing wax.

As Bob opened the tub Benjamin was reminded of how much he loved the way the wax smelled—a mixture of coconut milk and almond oil. He breathed it in and was suddenly filled with an inexplicable sense of comfort and familiarity. *Why was that?* Benjamin wondered for a second. Coconuts, almonds . . . what was it about that mixture that made him feel so good? His mind wandered. Was it something from childhood? Some suntan lotion he'd used on a family vacation?

His mind filled with a variety of images as he tried to place the scent. Almonds . . . coconuts . . . coconuts . . . almonds . . . and then all of a sudden he realized what it was: Nina. It was Nina. A few months ago she'd gone to the mall and bought a facial cleanser. It was made of a variety of tropical ingredients. Benjamin had loved its odor, but she had complained. "I smell like the glaze you'd put on one of those roasted pigs. Just put an apple in my mouth and skewer me!" she'd cracked. Benjamin smiled.

"That babe makes me smile, too," Bob said out of the blue.

"Huh?" Benjamin said. How did Bob know what he was thinking? "That babe!" Bob said, pointing a few feet in front of them. "You were staring at her and smiling."

"I—I—I was?" Benjamin asked. He hadn't recalled seeing anything but water in front of him.

"You don't have to be embarrassed, dude. She's a hottie if I ever saw one," Bob replied, slapping Benjamin on the back. "In fact, I think she just smiled at you."

"Really?" Benjamin squinted to get a closer look. There indeed was a girl standing not twenty feet in front of him. As far as Benjamin could tell, she was what Bob termed "a hottie." Blond hair, tan skin, and limbs that stretched on for days.

"She's waving to you, man!" Bob said. "You could at least wave back."

Benjamin waved. He could feel his cheeks flushing. "Go and talk to her, man," Bob cajoled. "Don't worry about me. You can leave me here."

"Uh, that's all right," Benjamin replied, his head still brimming with thoughts of Nina. "I'll talk to her later."

"Waves come first, right?" Bob answered, slapping Benjamin on the back again.

Benjamin shrugged. "Um . . . always!" he said.

"Well, let's go, then," Bob clamored, standing up and handing Benjamin the newly waxed board. Benjamin's nostrils were awash once again with the scent. *Don't think about Nina,* he instructed himself. *Remember: It's over.*

"Let's hit it, dude," Bob said, taking a towel and wiping down his own blue-and-white board.

"I'm with you," Benjamin replied.

Benjamin pressed his body flat against the board as he paddled out to sea. Everything seemed a little blurry to him. He fought a rising irritation with his sunglasses. *I've got to get a new pair,* Benjamin scoffed.

"Dude, here's where we stop," Bob called. "There's some wicked action out there today. With your scratchy board you gotta be careful."

"Just a little bit more!" Benjamin called back.

"Dude, no way," Bob called out again. "I'm serious. The sun rays must be getting to your head! It's too rough out there!"

It wasn't like Bob to be this tentative. *Could it be that I've graduated beyond Bob's level?* Benjamin wondered. *I mean, I know my board is a little messed up, but I'll be cool. It's not like there are even any big waves.*

Benjamin began his descent farther out into the ocean. It seemed tranquil as he paddled outward. Surfers always said you never knew when a big one was coming; sometimes the ocean could feel really calm, and all of a sudden a huge one would hit. Benjamin didn't think about that as he headed seaward. It was so bright out, all he could see ahead of him were dazzling patches of sunlight.

It wasn't until Benjamin had gotten a couple of feet out that he heard the cacophony of voices. "Dude, this one's like the big kahuna," someone screamed. It sounded like Bob.

Benjamin was confused. He hadn't felt anything. And he hadn't seen anything.

Benjamin barely had time to take position before the big wave came. *How could I not have felt this coming?* Benjamin thought. *How could I not have seen this coming?*

Benjamin was trying to come up with some answers when the wave hit. He rode the wave for about a fifth of a second. And then it was all a big blur.

It wasn't that Lucas didn't appreciate his mother's words of wisdom, it was just that he didn't really want to hear them early in the morning. Mostly when he'd already been at work for four hours and was coming home for a much needed break.

"And another thing, Lucas. You have to remember to wear sunscreen. Your father always bought his at the drugstore. The generic brand. Nothing fancy."

Lucas nodded as he slathered a piece of sourdough toast with butter and took a bite. Since his father's death his mother had become a lot more outspoken. She was always voicing concern about one thing or another.

"Do you know what kind I'm talking about, Lucas?" his mother asked him as she poured herself a second cup of coffee. He pointed to his full mouth so his mother knew that the only reason he wasn't responding was that he was busy chewing.

"Sorry," she said. "You're right. You should eat up. You still have half of the workday ahead of you."

Lucas nodded as he took a sip of orange juice and glanced at his waterproof digital watch. It had been his father's. Seven thirty-five A.M., almost time to make his way back to the docks. To start another work shift full of live bait, lobster entrails, and old fishermen who spent their days riffing on tourists and complaining about the "old lady." *I fit right in,* he thought dryly.

"Another thing, Lucas," his mother added. "Remember to save all the receipts when you go to the supply store today. I have to bring everything to the accountant the day after tomorrow. You know I loved your father, but he left the books such a mess."

"I know, Mom." Lucas said, brushing crumbs off the front of his shirt as he stood up. He walked over to her and kissed her on the cheek. She smelled like cold cream.

"You're a good boy, Lucas," his mom said. "Take your windbreaker just in case."

"I will," Lucas replied. "I'll be home for dinner."

"Don't feel obligated, honey," his mom added.

"What do you mean?" Lucas asked. That was strange. These days his mom was pretty set on family dinners, although the only additional member of the family was their boarder and family friend, Kate Levin.

"Well, I know Zoey's back in town," his mom said. "Kate mentioned that she was going to a surprise party to welcome her home."

"Oh, well, I'll still be back for dinner," Lucas stammered. "Don't worry, Mom."

"Okay, but if you want to see Zoey, I understand," his mom said.

"No, I don't," Lucas said. His mom looked at him strangely. That had come out wrong; so wrong, it almost stunned Lucas. Of course he wanted to see Zoey. He loved her—more than anything else in the world. "I mean," Lucas began again, "I want to see Zoey, but I want to have dinner with you, too."

"What a sweet thing to say, Lucas," his mom said, clearly pleased. "Don't forget your lunch."

Lucas paused before he grabbed the red-and-black-checkered plastic thermos and the brown paper bag. He remembered the countless times his father had made the same motion. "This minestrone?" his dad would ask as he slipped the thermos in the front pocket of his bulky jacket. "Yes, dear," his mother would answer. Unless, of course, it was split pea or tomato. It rarely was, though. Minestrone had been his dad's favorite.

"Have a good day," his mother said as she smiled at him. Lucas slipped on his windbreaker and watched out of the corner of his eye as his mother began brewing another pot of coffee. She was probably waiting for Kate to get up.

Lucas trudged out of the house, the thick rubber soles of his work boots making a sloshing sound in the grass. "Another day, another dollar," he could hear his dad mutter. Lucas remembered the first time he'd heard his dad say that. He'd been struck by how depressing it was. Was that all life was? Getting by? "That's not going to be me," Lucas had sworn to himself at the time. But now it was him. He was a Chatham Island fisherman, and he'd never be anything else. He wouldn't be going to college like everyone else. He'd be stuck on the island forever.

Lucas had a sudden urge to stop the train of miserable thoughts. The last thing he needed to do was spend the morning brooding over his hopeless future. He continued walking as he reached into his backpack and pulled out his Discman. Music would help.

Lucas slipped the headphones over his head and turned the volume up to eight. The sounds of Blur overpowered him. "They're just a cheap imitation of Pavement," Nina had said of the band. Lucas chuckled at the thought of the only bright spot the last few weeks had held: his friendship with Nina Geiger.

Who would have thought that he could find comfort in her company? Weird, neurotic Nina. She was always dyeing her hair, always eating something strange, always slacking around in some bizarre pair of overalls, or army fatigues, or painter's pants with frayed bottoms. Until a few days ago Lucas had seen his girlfriend's best friend as an amusing character—not much more.

How weird it was to think that everything could change so quickly. When Zoey left for Washington, Lucas and Nina had hung out. Mainly they'd talked. Nina had opened up to Lucas about her problems with Benjamin. Lucas had confided his feelings about work and his family to Nina. With Zoey gone, Nina was the only person on the island who didn't make him feel completely disconnected, completely isolated, completely alone. She could be so funny and relaxed. It rubbed off on him.

Lucas knew that all Zoey wanted was for him to be friends with Nina. That was so very Zoey: to want everyone she loved to love one another. Maybe it was the result of growing up with hippie parents; Lucas wasn't sure. All he knew was that his girlfriend was always throwing parties, always trying to get the gang together, always trying to achieve some sort of harmony among her friends.

But boy, had he and Nina found harmony.

Lucas actually paused in his walk as he thought about the kiss he and Nina had shared. It was one of the biggest mistakes he'd ever made. Because now—no matter how soothing a presence Nina could be for him—he couldn't indulge himself. They'd passed the stage of "hanging out as friends." With the kiss they'd crossed the line. And although Lucas needed Nina as a friend now more than ever, he was afraid there was no turning back.

It was all a big mess.

Lucas turned up the volume on his Discman to ten and continued his walk toward the docks. He tried not to think about anything.

Lara emptied her purse. Scattered on her unmade bed were receipts, gum wrappers, an old dried-up white frosted lipstick, two worn-down black eyeliners, a crumpled-up letter from a creepy guy she'd met at the rehab center, a book of matches from a bar she used to go to in Boston, and a mess of crumbs from a package of age-old peanut butter and cheese crackers.

Nothing that she needed.

"Gross," Lara groused as she swept the crumbs off

the sheet with the back of her hand. All this mess, and she didn't have a thing to show for it. Not to mention the fact that searching her bag had been her last hope, the beacon of light in the search for loose change.

Lara had spent the past few hours in the pursuit of stray coinage. She'd gone through the pockets of every pair of jeans she'd worn for the past week; she'd crammed her hand between the cushions of her beat-up old couch; she'd even slid belly-up under the bed. So far she'd come up with two dollars and twenty-five cents. That was maybe enough for a Coke and some chips.

Lara was very annoyed. She had convinced her father to let her work a shift at the restaurant, but she wasn't assigned until the next day, and she was completely out of cash.

"This is just my luck," Lara grumbled as she slung her purse over her shoulder and slipped on her sneakers. "A day off and no money."

Lara shuffled down Center Street, her loose change jingling in the front pocket of her red denim miniskirt. "Coffee, I need coffee," she mumbled as she tramped along.

Lara figured she'd go to Burger Heaven. They had the cheapest jolt of java on the island. Of course, it might mean running into Jake and his loser girlfriend, Kate Levin, but she'd live. Lara didn't really care about Jake anymore. She was way beyond that.

Dock Street was crowded with people. "Move!" Lara snarled as she wove through a mass of preteen girls. "You could get out of my way this year," she moaned as an old couple strolled toward her on the narrow walkway. Sometimes Lara got an incredible sense of power from being as scary as possible.

She was nearing Burger Heaven when a group of boys flew past her on their skateboards. "Hey!" Lara barked. "Watch where you're going!" As she was midyelp, another set of boys followed, only they were on in-line skates.

"Outta the way, lady!" one of them screeched as he careened toward her. Before Lara knew it, she was splayed out on the ground. "Sorry!" the kid yelled over his shoulder, but he was already a block away. "You'd better be glad you're going so fast, or you'd be dead at a young age!" Lara shouted as she brushed the soot off her skirt and stood up. "Get me some caffeine. Now."

The smell of grease overpowered her as she opened the door to Burger Heaven. Lara took a seat at the counter. Maybe she'd have a piece of pie, too. She felt like she deserved it. So what if she'd have no money for later? Anyway, all she felt like doing was taking a nap.

Lara reached into her pocket and grabbed for the change. She was stunned. There was only fifty cents left. That wasn't even enough for coffee. Lara stood up and made a lunge for the door. All her money must have fallen out of her pocket when she'd been nearly killed by those juvenile delinquents!

"Now I'll have to scrounge around the street for the coins," Lara told herself. "How humiliating," she mumbled.

But when Lara got outside, the street was packed once again. "Hey, look, Ma, I found a quarter!" a little kid screamed. "And another one!"

Lara watched in horror as a small tourist kid picked up her loose change coin by coin.

If it were one of the teenagers, Lara would just have grabbed it back. But even she wouldn't stoop to beating up a little kid for a quarter.

This was just her luck.

Christopher

<u>LIES</u>

AISHA DOESN'T GET IT. SHE THINKS I'M LYING TO HER. BUT THERE ARE MANY DIFFERENT KINDS OF TRUTH.

I GUESS THAT DOESN'T MAKE MUCH SENSE. IT'S KIND OF THE DIFFERENCE BETWEEN "THE GLASS IS HALF FULL" AND "THE GLASS IS HALF EMPTY." IT'S ALL ABOUT HOW YOU LOOK AT SOMETHING. IT'S CALLED PERSPECTIVE.

I WISH AISHA WOULD LOOK AT THINGS FROM MY PERSPECTIVE.

THIS IS THE WAY IT IS: I LOVE AISHA GRAY.

THAT IS THE TRUTH. THE REST OF MY LIFE —EVERYTHING THAT WENT ON BEFORE I MET HER —JUST DOESN'T MATTER ANYMORE. IT'S LIKE IT HAPPENED TO A DIFFERENT PERSON.

AND I DON'T WANT AISHA TO GET TO KNOW THAT PERSON. WHY SHOULD SHE? HE DOESN'T EVEN EXIST ANYMORE.

I DON'T WANT AISHA TO JUDGE ME ON THE BASIS OF SOMEONE I USED TO BE. I DON'T WANT TO LOSE HER OVER SOMETHING I'VE DONE THAT I ALREADY REGRET.

THIS IS THE WAY I SEE THE GLASS OF

WATER: It doesn't matter if it's half full or half empty. When you've had a life like mine, you learn that what is important is that it's yours, and you'd better drink that water down before anyone tries to take it away from you.

JAKE

Lies

Kate thought that once I found out that she's a depressive, I'd end our relationship. But who understands more about depression than I do?

I was depressed when my brother died.

I was depressed when Zoey Passmore dumped me for Lucas.

I was depressed when I discovered I was an alcoholic.

I was depressed during my "relationship" with Lara McAvoy.

So it's not like I don't understand about Kate. I do.

I just think that she should acknowledge she has a problem. Stop blaming her mother, start going to therapy more, stop forgetting to take her medication.

If there's one thing I learned in A.A., it's that—although it seems like living the lie is easier than living the truth, it never is.

In the end the lies come back to you.

Three

The cordless phone next to Claire's bed let out a vicious squeal.

At least Claire knew that it wasn't the stalker calling.

That was the one progressive step she'd taken last week: getting the Geiger number changed. She'd told her family that she was sick of the crank phone calls they'd been getting. She'd expected them to argue, but none had—at least not too ferociously. Generally speaking, people avoided arguing with Claire. She could be very unpleasant when she didn't get her way.

After her night of no sleep Claire had no desire to speak to anyone on the phone. "I am *not* answering it," she grumbled.

It kept ringing.

Claire figured that it was a business associate of her dad's or one of Sarah's friends. The last thing in the world she wanted to do was be polite to someone she barely knew. Talking to her dad's associate about the upcoming company picnic or listening to Mrs. So-and-so from the board of the such-and-such charity spout off on how absolutely darling Sarah had been to attend the such-and-such luncheon in honor of Mr. and Mrs. So-and-so.

Claire didn't think either of those conversations would do much to improve her mental state.

Then again, it could be Aaron. Claire doubted it. Her boyfriend's calls were few and far between these days, what with him on the road with his band and all.

"Someone pick it up. Please, someone pick it up," Claire mumbled under her breath. The ringing hurt her ears.

Still no one answered it. Claire figured that probably everyone in the house was either gone or—in the case of Nina—home but still barely awake.

Finally Claire heard the answering machine turn on. It was Nina's voice. "Hello, you've reached *us*. That's Burke, Sarah, Claire, and Nina. If you are trying to sell *us* something, please begin speaking now and hang up at the tone. All others please begin speaking at the tone and hang up when you are finished."

Claire hated it when Nina left such bizarre messages. "Why does everything you do have to be weird?" she'd argued. "Can't you just do something the normal way for once in your life?"

Claire listened as another beep went off and the tape started to roll. There was a bit of static, a tiny bit of breathing, and then silence. Finally there was a click as the caller hung up.

"I hate hang ups," Claire mumbled. "What do people think we bought the answering machine for?"

Claire pulled the covers over her head. She was completely exhausted. Maybe she'd try to get a little sleep.

But the phone started ringing again.

Zoey had shown up at Lucas's house only to be informed that she'd just missed him. "I'm surprised you didn't see him walking out," Mrs. Cabral said.

Mrs. Cabral had offered Zoey a cup of coffee, but

41

she'd declined. "I want to see if I can find Lucas," she'd chirped, and hurried off.

Zoey's jogging shoes made a slapping sound on the muddy walkway as she trotted down Center Street en route to the docks. At every corner she expected to see Lucas. *He must walk faster than I jog,* Zoey thought.

Finally she saw him. He was walking steadily toward the boat, his back to her. He looked broad under the windbreaker and the various layers of clothes. Bigger. Formidable.

"Lucas!" Zoey called out. "Lucas!" He didn't turn around.

She ran a bit closer until she was no more than two feet away. "Lucas!" she screamed.

He still didn't turn around.

He was completely oblivious to her presence.

Claire was becoming increasingly annoyed. Whoever was calling refused to leave a message. The person had called three times. They'd listened to the outgoing message three times. They'd hung up three times.

At least I know it's not the stalker, Claire thought. Because there's no way that he could get this phone number.

The phone started ringing again.

Zoey surprised Lucas by running up behind him and grabbing him around the waist.

It had been a tactical error. He'd been wearing a Discman, and she'd caught him so off guard, he'd nearly jumped two feet in the air. A thermos he'd been carrying in his jacket front pocket went flying, minestrone soup spilling everywhere, and his Discman loosened itself from his headphones, opening and falling to the ground. The CD fell out.

"Jesus, Zoey," Lucas nearly shouted as he picked up the soup-covered CD from the ground. "I had no idea you were there."

"I've been screaming to you for the past few minutes," Zoey said apologetically. "Oh, I'm so sorry, Lucas." She used the corner of her T-shirt to wipe off the minestrone on his windbreaker. "I don't think that's going to stain," she added.

"Whatever," he mumbled. "It doesn't matter, Zo."

"Well, I just wanted to say hi to you," Zoey murmured. She dabbed at his windbreaker a bit more. "You can't blame a girl for that," she added hopefully, wiping the last spot of soup off his jacket and giving him a kiss on the cheek.

"I'm not mad," Lucas replied, his eyes darting around nervously. Zoey had the distinct impression her boyfriend didn't want to look at her.

But why would that be?

The phone was ringing. Again. This time Claire picked it up after one ring. "Hello!" she answered. "Hello?"

There was a quick breath and then a click.

Claire's stomach lurched. *It feels like old times,* she thought.

But how? How in the world had the stalker gotten the new number?

"Lucas, are you in a bad mood?" Zoey asked. The minute the words were out of her mouth, she felt like slapping herself on the forehead. That was always the wrong thing to ask. It was one of those questions that tended to answer itself, because the minute you asked someone if they were in a bad mood, they got into one. But there was no taking it back now.

"No, I . . . I just don't want to go back to work, that's all," Lucas mumbled as an excuse.

"Oh, well, don't worry," Zoey comforted. "It'll all be over soon."

Lucas gave her a weird look. "What do you mean?" he asked.

"I mean," Zoey replied, "that it'll all be over. Soon you won't have to work on the boat because you'll be at college."

"Zo," Lucas stumbled. "I—I—I guess I haven't told you yet. My mom says I'm not going to be able to go to college next semester. I gotta work on the boat."

"Oh, Lucas!" Zoey cried sympathetically. "I'm so sorry!"

"Well, it's not so bad," Lucas mumbled. "I'm going to try to get a deferment."

"That's good," Zoey said, "but still."

"But still what?" Lucas asked. Zoey could hear a tinge of defensiveness in his voice.

"But I know you don't want to be doing this," Zoey responded. She didn't know what else to say.

"What difference does it make where I am?" Lucas asked. "I mean, you're going to be in California."

"Lucas," Zoey cried. "It matters because I want you to be happy! I can't be happy if you're not happy!"

"You don't have to pity me," Lucas said sharply.

"I'm not pitying you," Zoey replied, although she could tell from the disgruntled look on his face that Lucas didn't believe her. He was so easily offended sometimes, but he looked particularly fragile now. Not angry, really. Just upset.

"I gotta go," Lucas said somewhat abruptly. "I gotta be on the boat in a second."

"Lucas," Zoey cried. "Please, let's finish this. You

44

need someone to talk to about everything! I feel like I've barely seen you! I feel like—"

Lucas cut her off. "Zoey, you've been in town less than a day. We'll catch up later," he said brusquely. He gave her a quick kiss on the cheek.

Suddenly Zoey was standing on the street by herself. She could still feel the kiss.

The phone rang again. Claire didn't even bother to say hello this time. She just picked up the phone and hung up on the caller. She knew who it was. It was him. It had to be.

To say that Claire was freaked out would be an understatement of enormous proportions.

When the phone rang again, she decided to just take the whole thing off the hook.

Doing so made her feel like she was giving up, but she absolutely wasn't. She just didn't know what to do. Yet.

Zoey began her walk back home, wondering how and why things could have gone so awry with Lucas when she hadn't even been home for twenty-four hours.

Zoey's mind was racing, but she knew she'd better not overanalyze the situation. Nina was always telling her she read too much into things. "You don't only read between the lines, you read over the lines, under the lines, and above the lines," Nina had once teased her.

The sun was out now, and Zoey watched as Chatham Island began to glow with daylight. It was weird to think of Lucas here without her. She'd imagined them both going off to college and coming home for vacations at the same time. She'd imagined them taking a walk around the island, holding hands and exclaiming things like: "I can't believe we've been gone for so long! It's like we never left! Doesn't it seem like nothing's changed?"

But Lucas wouldn't be leaving Chatham Island. He'd be here in the fall. And in the winter and spring, too. Yet another reason for him to befriend Nina, Zoey reasoned. Nina still had another year of high school left, and she was always complaining that she was being abandoned. "Left to rot like road pizza," was the way she put it. *Other than Nina, there's really not going to be anyone our age left on the island,* Zoey contemplated. Everyone else would be gone. Zoey thought through the list of friends. Eesh was going to be at Princeton, Claire at MIT, Benjamin at Columbia, Aaron at Harvard, Jake at the University of Massachusetts. There was Kate. That would be good for Lucas. When she'd first moved to town, Zoey had feared that Lucas had been into Kate in a romantic way, but it turned out they were more like family than anything else. So Kate would be around. And Nina. That was it.

And, of course, Lucas.

Four

Lara watched intently as Zoey walked along the docks.

Lara held the palm of her right hand over her nose and inhaled. Her hands smelled like a combination of aloe vera lotion and turpentine. It wasn't the most savory of smells, but it was better than the fishy scents that wafted in the air. Lara was never sure how Chatham Island's residents got used to the odor. It made her want to puke.

Lara had been up late painting, and she had used the turpentine to get the oily pigment stains off her hands. She was working on a series of paintings based on a set of cheeseball touristy postcards someone had left behind at the Passmores' restaurant. Lara knew she should have put the postcards in the restaurant's lost-and-found box, but she hadn't. Why not? As she saw it: Anybody rich enough to eat lobster for lunch could afford to buy another set of dumb postcards.

Anyway, dorky as they were, the colorized images of sunsets over the cliffs, proud old fishermen holding up lobsters, and happy tourists ambling around The Hub had inspired her. She'd begun painting the same scenes, only hers were infused with a dark irony. She used drab colors—olive green, mustard yellow, muddy pink—where the postcards used bright ones. The faces of Lara's fishermen wore frowns and had dark circles

47

under their eyes. Her sunsets were weighted down under a foggy mist; the air looked dirty and polluted.

Lara's Chatham Island was an ugly place.

Sometimes Lara would lie in bed and wonder what her life would have been like had she grown up on Chatham Island with her father, Jeff Passmore, and not in Boston with her mom. Quaint, precious Chatham Island. What if she'd been raised here? Would she still have all her artistic aspirations?

I'm better off with the life I've had was what Lara usually rationalized. *Hard as it's been, at least it's been interesting. I never would have become an artist if I'd grown up here. You need angst for art*, Lara told herself. *I mean, if I'd grown up here, I could have ended up boring, precious, and smug like . . . Zoey.*

At the thought of her simpering half sister Lara focused in on the real purpose of her early morning excursion: her scheme du jour—to break up Zoey and her boyfriend, Lucas.

Ever since Lara had moved to the island, she'd been aware—acutely aware—that Zoey Passmore didn't like her. Correction: that Zoey Passmore completely resented her. Correction: that Zoey Passmore totally couldn't stand the sight of her.

Well, Lara was going to give her a good reason to hate her. *Wait until I separate her from her beloved little Lucas!* Lara thought merrily. *She doesn't know hatred!*

Lara had been on her way to the Passmores' house this morning (nothing like a free cup of coffee) when she'd seen Zoey leave the house. She'd been surprised at her good luck and decided to follow her. Keeping ten steps back, Lara watched from a distance as Zoey scampered over to Lucas's house, found him not home, and walked toward the docks. Then she'd observed Zoey and Lucas's exchange. She'd laughed mockingly when Zoey practically knocked Lucas over, spilling soup all over his jacket, and she'd smiled wryly when Lucas gave Zoey what seemed to her to be a kiss on the cheek good-bye.

A kiss on the cheek? That seemed a bit odd. Even for Mr. and Mrs. Innocence.

Could it be there was already trouble in paradise?

Maybe Lara's job was going to be a lot easier than she'd expected.

When Claire was confident that her father and stepmother had left the house, she got out of bed. Her legs wobbled when her bare feet hit the floor.

Claire stumbled from her bed to her closet and grabbed the blue-and-white-striped terry cloth robe that hung from a hook on the side of the door. The robe had been a gift from Sarah when Claire was accepted into MIT. At the time she'd accepted a present from her stepmother begrudgingly—now she really liked the robe. It was soft and thick, and warm enough to wear outside on the widow's walk above her room, where Claire often went to think.

Claire slipped her long arms into the sleeves of the robe, one at a time. When she had it on, she went to grab her slippers. It was when she looked down that she realized there was a problem, a big one: The robe had been cut off at the midriff.

Claire stifled a scream. "This guy must have used gardening shears," she growled, fingering the frayed bottom of the ultrathick fabric.

Aside from the half a robe, Claire was wearing a Calvin Klein tank top and underwear set. She'd had them on underneath the dress she'd worn to Zoey's last night, and she'd slept in them. She looked down at the dress from last night—it lay crumpled on the floor. Claire contemplated putting it back on, but it was a little dressy for everyday. Even for her.

No, she needed to find an entirely new set of clothes

to put on. Where could she get them? Claire could peruse Sarah Mendel's wardrobe, but she didn't think a lavender tweed suit with brass buttons from the Talbots catalog would really be appropriate. She could go into her dad's closet and try to create a men's dress shirt/men's chinos ensemble, although it'd be difficult, considering Burke Geiger's ever expanding waistline. Or she could do the unthinkable. The unmentionable. The un-everything-able.

She could borrow clothes from—gasp, shudder—Nina.

It was horrible to think about, but what other choice did she have?

Claire stomped down the hall toward her sister's room. The door was closed, but she didn't hesitate to bang on it with her closed fist. This was an emergency, after all, and Nina was a notoriously deep sleeper.

"That outfit isn't working for you, Claire," Nina muttered bitterly when she finally came to the door. She held it halfway open so that Claire could catch a glimpse of the mess of papers, magazines, clothes, makeup, and CDs. Such was Nina's decorating concept.

"I really don't need you to *House of Style* me, Nina," Claire retorted. "I just need to borrow some clothes."

Nina stood there a minute, her mouth hanging open. Then she recovered herself. "What's wrong with yours?" she asked, raising an eyebrow suspiciously.

Claire wasn't prepared for this. "Uh, they're in the laundry," she stumbled.

"And what happened to your robe?" Nina continued, clearly starting to wake up. "Or is that an Edward Scissorhands exclusive?"

Claire scowled. "Aren't we witty first thing in the morning? Let's just say it came upon a bit of an accident," she responded obliquely. She was eager to get this over with, and Nina wasn't making it easy.

Thankfully Nina's laziness got the better of her. "Whatever you say." She shrugged hopelessly, opening the door to her room all the way and pointing Claire in the direction of the closet. "Do your damage," she instructed. "I'm going back to bed."

Half an hour later, Nina was snoring and Claire had finally assembled an outfit that worked for her. Well, kind of worked for her. Picking an outfit from Miss Wannabe Riot Grrrl's closet had certainly been a challenge—not only because most of the contents of her closet were winter wear and it was now summer but also because Claire was practically a head taller than Nina and narrower as well. Claire had sifted through the gaudy polyester pants, tentlike thrift store dresses, and oversize men's sweaters and come up with as simple a concoction as possible: a plaid miniskirt with a black button-up. The skirt was a little too short and it had a coffee stain on the front, and the black button-up was actually an old bowling shirt that Nina had stolen from Weymouth Lanes, but the outfit was passable. Sort of. It would take Claire through the day at least. She'd have to go to the mall later.

"Only my sister could go into my closet and come out looking like a uniformed schoolgirl," Nina grumbled from her bed.

"Thanks . . . I guess," Claire responded.

"I was hoping you'd come up with something a little more dangerous," Nina commented. "Are you sure you don't want to wear my Marilyn Manson concert T-shirt?"

Claire shook her head no—*dangerous* was a word she wanted to avoid.

Claire was halfway out the door when Nina shouted, "Hey, can you leave that half a robe for me? I think I can make some leg warmers out of it. Wouldn't that be rad?"

Claire let the door slam behind her.

Five

Kate felt like she was percolating. She'd had two cups of coffee with Mrs. Cabral at breakfast, and then she'd taken a walk to Burger Heaven to grab a cup of coffee to go. She was just procrastinating; it wasn't like she'd needed that third cup of the day. But, well, she hadn't felt like working. And anyway, her boyfriend, Jake, worked at Burger Heaven. What better way to get inspired than to see him?

Of course, Jake had been busy. Too busy to hang out with her. He'd barely had time to talk to her, really. And it didn't help that his boss was standing over them the whole time. Kate couldn't see why Max gave Jake such a hard time. Jake was such a good worker. And ever since Max had accused Jake of taking too many breaks, she'd tried to keep herself scarce at Burger Heaven. She still felt bad about that.

Kate was in the darkroom now. She used wooden clothespins to fasten the developing photos to white clotheslines strung across the ceiling. Kate had learned to be meticulous about labeling her photographs, and she kept a notebook next to her at all times in which she listed the numbers of the prints with descriptions of the content.

Photo 1181	Jake at work
Photo 1182	Jake on football field
Photo 1183	Lucas and Mrs. Cabral eat dinner
Photo 1184	Mom visits (out of focus)
Photo 1185	Mom visits (overexposed)
Photo 1186	Jake at home
Photo 1187	Jake on the rocks

Kate inspected Photo 1187. There was something incredibly simple in Jake's expression. His gaze, the way his eyes met the camera, was just uncomplicated. It was like all his emotions were in order.

To Kate, Jake's photo signified his strength. Since her relapse of depression, that was exactly what Kate felt she needed. At least Kate could take solace in the fact that her mother had gone back to New York. Kate couldn't imagine she'd be hearing from dear old mom anytime soon, especially considering the letter she'd sent her. Regret was an emotion that was very familiar to Kate, but she didn't think that she'd regret sending that letter. In it she'd accused her mother of trying to ruin her relationship with Jake. Kate knew that she was right, and now she wanted nothing to do with her mom.

It was kind of a relief, really. Gone were the daily nagging phone calls. Gone were the countless messages on the machine reminding Kate to take her medication. Gone were the harassing visits.

Yes, Kate's mom was gone from her life. And Kate was relieved. She really was.

Wasn't she?

Kate glanced at her watch. Only a few more hours until Jake was off work.

She could make it until then.

At least she hoped she could.

Nina stuck her head under the bed. "Lint much?" she muttered as she felt around the dark clutter for the lost item. "This is so annoying," she said to no one in particular. "Why am I such a hideous mess?"

Nina couldn't for the life of her remember where she'd put her Blur CD, but she'd woken up with the sudden desperate urge to listen to it. "They're just a cheap imitation of Pavement," she grumbled to herself. "I don't know why I want to hear them so badly. They must have been in my dream or something." Nina pulled her head out from under the bed. She stayed sitting Indian style in the middle of the room. *Could it be that I threw it out?* she asked herself. *Or maybe Claire has it?* "Yeah, right," Nina growled. "Like Claire would take my Blur CD." Claire would never listen to an alternative rock band. She was Miss Mainstream. "You're so Sheryl Crow," Nina was always taunting her.

Nina sighed. *Maybe I'll get lucky and their video will be on MTV,* she thought, searching amidst the piles of magazines, dirty clothes, and empty crumpled bags of salt and vinegar potato chips (they'd been out of sour cream and onion at the store) for the remote control. "Here, clicker, clicker, clicker," she purred. "Come to Mama!"

Nina found the remote control under a wet towel, which she tossed toward the hamper. The buttons felt slimy when she touched them. She pressed ninety-six for MTV.

"Oh, yippee, another episode of *Road Rules*," Nina growled, disappointed. "Doesn't the *M* in MTV stand for music?"

Annoyed, Nina was about to turn the power off, but then she reconsidered. *What better way to start the day?* she thought. A little morning channel surfing never hurt anyone. After all, what else did she have to do?

People were always saying that channel flipping was the domain of bored sports-addicted husbands, but Nina prided herself on being quite the expert little flipper. For instance, she could guess a talk show topic in a matter of seconds even when she tuned in halfway through.

Surf's up, Nina thought as she began flipping through the channels. She went from talk show to talk show. "My Boyfriend Has a Weight Problem!" she barked. "My Kid Was Burned by Show Business!" she cried. "I'm Addicted to Soap Operas!" she called.

Nina was awed by her own uncanny powers as she flipped to another station. There were a bunch of women sitting onstage, hurling insults at each other, and the host was trying to calm them down. "Ladies, ladies," she was calling out. "Let's have some order." *Oh, this is an easy one,* Nina thought, giving the group of cackling females the once-over. *They do this one all the time.* But just as she was about to guess "Kleptomaniac Love Addicts Who Think They're All That," the host turned to the audience.

"And we'll be back," she announced exuberantly, "with today's topic: 'I'm in Love with My Best Friend's Boyfriend.'"

Nina's stomach lurched, and she thought she could feel the potato chips she'd eaten last night come up her throat. She knew there'd been something she'd been avoiding thinking about all morning: Lucas.

Lucas, Lucas, Lucas. Hadn't it only been a few days ago that Nina had thought she'd never be able to get over her relationship with Benjamin? And now the whole escapade, the whole affair had been eclipsed. By Lucas.

She wasn't sure what was preferable: complete heartbreak or total unrequited longing. *Could my love life be in any more of a shambles?* Nina thought mournfully. *It's over with Benjamin, and it will never be with Lucas.*

The commercial break ended.

"And we're back," the host announced. "With more about being in love with your best friend's boyfriend."

Nina lunged for the remote. She scanned the channels in search of suitable viewing material, something more innocuous. She settled for figure-skating championships on SportsChannel.

She watched as the perfect little girls in ridiculous outfits jumped around. *They look like little aliens,* Nina thought spitefully. Unfortunately, as absurdly mind numbing as their choreographed efforts were, they weren't enough to keep Nina from thinking about Lucas.

As far as Nina was concerned, last night's welcome-home party for Zoey had been a complete fiasco. Not because anything *bad* had actually happened. Zoey had seemed thrilled to be home, and no scandals took place. It was just that Nina had felt bad the entire time. She'd felt phony, horrible, practically evil. After all, only two days before she'd kissed Lucas. And, of course, Lucas was Zoey's boyfriend. Nina shuddered at the thought. She'd always prided herself on being someone who would always put friendship in front of anything, and here she'd gone and kissed her best friend's boyfriend when her best friend was away. She was scum. No, she was worse than scum, she was algae! No, she was worse than algae! But what was worse than algae?

Nina contemplated retrieving her ninth-grade biology textbook from the shelf so she could find out what was lower on the food chain than algae, but a knock on the door derailed her. It had to be her sister. "No, Claire, you cannot borrow my combat boots to go with your outfit," Nina barked at the closed door.

"It's me, Zoey!" Nina heard from the other side of the door. "Can I come in?"

"S-S-Sure," Nina gasped. What was Zoey doing here? "But, uh, be warned. It's a little scary in here."

Zoey opened the door, and the dark room flooded with light. "Sorry to just show up," Zoey said. "I've been trying to call you for a while, but I kept getting a busy signal. I thought something was wrong."

"Claire took the phone off the hook," Nina said. "More crank calls, apparently." She cleared away some debris so that Zoey could sit next to her.

"Oh," Zoey said. Nina could hear a bit of something in her voice. Could it be that she knew?

"So what's up?" Nina asked, her gaze fixated on a particularly tiny ice skater's wobbly triple lutz. She looked like she was going to fall for a second, but she recovered her balance. Nina couldn't help feeling a bit disappointed.

"Well, I just saw Lucas," Zoey replied. Nina could hear the wistfulness in Zoey's voice. Her voice always got like that when she was upset.

She knows, Nina thought. *Oh, God, what am I going to do? She knows. Now she hates me, and I'll have to find a new best friend.*

"And?" Nina said, trying not to sound too nervous.

"And nothing . . . really," Zoey said tentatively. "It was just a little awkward, I guess."

Nina heaved a sigh of relief. Zoey didn't know. "Awkward? How?"

"Well, you know, he was going back to work, and I surprised him by showing up at his house. He wasn't there, so I met up with him near the docks. I don't know, maybe he was just preoccupied or something, but he just didn't really seem that happy to see me," Zoey said forlornly.

"Oh, Zo," Nina said encouragingly. "Lucas loves you. Of course he was happy to see you."

"I don't know, Nina," Zoey whispered. "That's nice of you to say and all, but he was acting so strange. He told me about not going to college next year, and he got all defensive about it. It was like he'd been keeping all of these things bottled up inside." Zoey stopped to catch her breath. Then she added: "Of course, the guy hasn't had anyone to talk to for days now. So who can blame him for being upset?"

Uh, correction, Nina thought, *he had me to talk to.* Nina couldn't help feeling a bit affronted. She and Lucas had had some great soul-searching talks when Zoey was away. Had they meant nothing to him? Of course, she didn't say anything. How could she?

The two girls sat in silence for a few seconds. Nina knew she had to say something supportive. "Zoey," she replied finally. "I told you Lucas loves you. Don't worry about this." She tried to make her tone as declarative as possible.

It must have worked because after a moment's pause for thought, Zoey peered up at Nina and said, "Oh, Nin, I'm sorry for being such a pain. I'm being crazy, right? Paranoid?"

Nina gave a definitive nod. "You're being positively loopy. Are you sure you're feeling well?" She reached over and jokingly placed her palm on Zoey's forehead.

"Actually, Doctor," Zoey replied, smiling, "I don't think I got enough sleep last night."

"Well, then, that's all it is," Nina responded. "Insomniacal delusions got the better of you. Take a quick nap and call me in the morning."

Zoey laughed. "I'm sorry to put you through this. Especially when you've got Benjamin on your mind." Nina shrugged. It wasn't exactly Benjamin who was on her mind. "And anyway," Zoey went on, "everything was pretty good with Lucas last night. It must have just been his mood this morning."

"What was good about last night?" Nina asked, although she had a feeling she didn't want to hear the answer.

Nina watched as Zoey's mouth curled into a little smile. "It's just when we kissed . . . I mean, it was as good as ever. That was still really passionate and everything."

"That's amazing, Zo," Nina heard herself saying. She felt like she was having an out-of-body experience. It was like she was behaving one way on the outside and feeling entirely differently on the inside. The thought of Lucas kissing Zoey made her feel nauseous. Without warning, Nina was filled with jealousy and rage. *You better get ahold of yourself,* she thought. *You are not allowed to be jealous of your best friend over* her *boyfriend.* She fixed her gaze once again on the skating competition. She had to change the subject.

"Where do those girls get their outfits? I mean, there must have been a feather and sequin sale at Frederick's of Hollywood," Nina commented.

Zoey laughed and grabbed for the remote. "Why are we watching this, anyway?" she asked with a giggle. "Aren't any of your beloved talk shows on?"

Six

Aisha could feel her anger grow with every click-click of her cork-soled flip-flops.

She walked steadily and speedily along Bristol Street. She rarely took this route home from the ferry landing. Usually she went the longer route, which meant walking along Dock Street until it met the beach and then turning onto Climbing Way. Dock Street was usually teeming with people, especially this time of year—tourists, kids, shoppers, ferry-goers. It was always full of noise and color, which Aisha usually appreciated. Especially after she'd spent all day working out equations in the astronomy workshop she attended two times a week. Hours upon hours spent trying to calculate the distance between planets and comets; it was usually a relief to be among people and voices, even if most of them belonged to annoying little kids who were begging their crabby-looking mothers for ice-cream cones.

But today Aisha couldn't deal with Dock Street. All that noise wasn't good for someone who felt like she might explode into little bits all over the pavement. Aisha knew what they said in all those women's magazines her mother subscribed to: Anger wasn't good for you. What was that article she'd recently read? About how angry women were more prone to breakouts?

Well, bring on the acne, Aisha thought. *Because I'm pissed.*

Aisha had used a rubber band she'd found in the lab to tie her curly black hair up in a ponytail, and she could feel the sun beating down on the back of her bare neck. She regretted wearing her long black skirt; it clung to her upper thighs. She never wore this skirt, but she hadn't done her laundry in a long time. She'd been occupied with other things. Rather, with other thing: Christopher.

How could he have lied to me like that? Aisha steamed. *He told me that picture of him and that girl was from a prom, when really it was from a wedding, and not just any wedding, but* his *wedding,* his *wedding? And then when I'd told him I knew he'd been married, he told me it was none of my business!*

Aisha thought back to the picture. She had looked at it so many times, she could describe everything about it. The way Christopher's lip curled upward in this lackadaisical smile; the way his tuxedo shirt hugged his wide chest. He looked so relaxed. So happy. So young.

Aisha gritted her teeth at the thought of the photo. She could think of nothing but the voice she'd heard on the phone yesterday.

"Hello, this is Carina Connelly, how can I help you?" Aisha had replayed the phone call in her head over and over again. "Hello, this is Carina Connelly, how can I help you?" Aisha'd hung up right then, but now she almost wished she hadn't. In fact, she'd spent most of the morning imagining things she could have said. Like: "I'll tell you how you can help me. You can tell me if you're the Carina Connelly who was once married to my fiancé, Christopher. You can tell me if you're the Carina Connelly who Christopher's sister,

Kendra, claims was a drug addict. Better yet, you can cease to exist!"

But Aisha hadn't said any of those things. All she'd done was hang up the phone. She hadn't learned anything more about the woman who had once occupied Christopher's heart and—she hated this thought—his bed. It made Aisha feel ill. Kendra had said Carina had beautiful long curls. Had Christopher played with her curly hair? Wrapping the ringlets around his thick fingers, staring into her eyes, and telling her dreamy stories about their future? Had he kissed her like he kissed Aisha? Had he spent hours upon hours decorating her face and neck with small, gentle, soft-lipped kisses?

How can I tell which things he's told me have been true? Aisha fumed. *How can I ever trust him?*

Yes, Aisha was angry. Really angry. The anger filled her veins and was coming out of her every pore, her every follicle. It was like nothing she'd ever felt before. This anger was all-consuming. It was powerful. It was energizing. Aisha felt motivated.

But to do what?

One, two, three, four, five, six. Jake needed to hold the sit-up for fourteen more seconds.

Seven, eight, nine. This was his last round of sit-ups for the day. Three sets of twenty, twenty seconds each.

Ten, eleven, twelve. The muscles in Jake's upper thighs felt tight. Maybe he'd done too many free weights this morning.

Thirteen, fourteen, fifteen. Jake's upper arms were sore, too. But that was from slinging burgers all day. Not from working out.

Sixteen, seventeen, eighteen. Jake breathed in deeply. Sometimes after a long day at Burger Heaven he could smell oil, fries, and burnt meat for hours after he'd left. It was like the smell followed him home.

Nineteen, twenty. He was done. Jake exhaled loudly and grabbed for the bottle of Power Surge. It was a bright yellowish drink, the color of the Hi-Liter he'd used in his American history textbook. Jake usually made it a point not to put things in his body that looked like toxic waste, but his coach had gotten him hooked on this drink. He'd said it was good for him. Something about replenishing electrolytes. Jake wasn't sure what electrolytes were, but he was pretty certain he didn't want to run out of them.

Jake stood up. He turned up the volume on his boom box. He knew what everyone said about those L.A. gangsta rappers, that they were murderers and stuff. He guessed that was true. Still, raps were excellent to work out to. He'd bought a bunch of CDs at the mall the other day. Some of them were a little too violent for his taste, but some of them—like Coolio—seemed innocuous enough.

Jake decided to listen to one more track before he went up to shower. He rapped along as well as a guy with very little rhythm could, taking breaks to swig back more Power Surge when he didn't know the words. Sitting on the workbench, Jake did mini leg lifts to stretch his worked-out muscles while he surveyed the makeshift workout room he'd created in the garage. There was a mat on the floor, some hand weights off to the side, and two dumbbells. Nothing fancy, but everything he needed.

When the track ended, Jake stood up and stretched. He was wet with perspiration, the Chicago Bulls T-shirt with cutoff sleeves sticking to his chest. He took a quick glance at his reflection in the mirror hanging on the garage wall. For a football player he wasn't an incredibly large guy, but he was well built. Each muscle was smooth and well-defined.

"Well, I see I came at the right time," purred a familiar voice. Jake whipped around. Kate Levin was standing in the doorway to the garage, her hands on her hips. She was wearing a white sundress, against which her long, thick red hair looked majestic. She was smiling. Kate looked gorgeous when she smiled, and just one look at her radiant face should have filled Jake with warmth and pride.

But these days Jake often felt uneasy in his girlfriend's presence. She was so up and down all the time—he could never predict how long her good moods would last. She seemed happy enough now. Her cheeks were flushed, her blue eyes were bright, and she was holding out her arms to him.

"How long have you been here?" he asked as he walked toward her.

"Not long," she replied. They were face-to-face now. Jake gave her a quick kiss on the lips.

"Is that all?" she teased.

"I'm all hot and sweaty," Jake answered.

"I can see that," Kate replied, taking her index finger and placing it on the center of Jake's chest.

Jake could feel Kate's touch all the way down to his feet. "I should go take a shower," he said.

"Need to cool off?" Kate whispered in his ear, giving him a quick kiss on the neck.

"Uh, yeah, I guess so," Jake mumbled as his face flushed with embarrassment. It wasn't like Kate to act this aggressively, but she'd been acting strange fairly often these days. He wanted to ask her if she'd remembered to take her medication today but thought that might trigger a mood change.

That was something he definitely wanted to avoid.

The air-conditioning in the Gray Inn gave Aisha a momentary sense of relief. She was about to climb the stairs to her room in order to try to find something more comfortable to put on when her little brother, Kalif, skidded out of the kitchen and into the front room on socked feet. Clad in an oversize football jersey and jean shorts, Kalif was clutching a mop, which served as a makeshift hockey stick. "Goal," he screamed as the hackey sack he used as a puck went flying through the air, nearly grazing Aisha on the right side of the head.

"Jesus, Kalif!" Aisha hissed. "What's wrong with you?"

"Sorry, Eesh," Kalif said. He seemed a bit taken aback by the strength of her reaction. "I—I—I didn't see you in here," he stammered.

"Obviously!" Aisha growled. "But what if I'd been a guest and not me? Then what?"

"I was just playing." Kalif shrugged. "All the guests are out. The Passmores' are having some two-for-one lobster lunch special at their restaurant."

"Good excuse," Aisha grumbled.

"I didn't mean to make you so mad," he added.

Aisha exhaled loudly. "It's okay, Kalif," she said. "You didn't make me mad." *I was mad already,* she wanted to say, but she didn't think pouring her heart out to her eleven-year-old brother was the smartest move.

"Oh," Kalif said.

Aisha could see she'd confused him. Oh, well. There was no way she could explain her mood to him. "I'm sorry for barking at you, baby bro," she said, trying to gentle her tone. "I've just had a hard day, that's all."

"I hate school, too," Kalif said empathetically.

Aisha gave a little laugh. "It's not school," she said. Sometimes Kalif was such a little kid.

"Oh, well, are you mad about having too many chores to do?" Kalif inquired. "'Cause chores make me pretty pissed off, too."

"No." Aisha laughed, putting her book bag down on the couch. She'd take it upstairs in a few minutes. "But speaking of chores," she said, "I guess it's time to get to mine. Is Mom around?"

"She went to the store," Kalif replied, crossing the front room to retrieve his hackey sack. "Kendra's in the kitchen, though."

Aisha nodded. Good. She needed to talk to Kendra. "Well, I'm going to go say hi to her," she said. Her flip-flops clicked especially loudly as she crossed the hardwood floors.

Kendra was sitting at the kitchen table, folding yellow-and-white-checkered cloth napkins. She was listening to the radio, singing along to a song Aisha recognized but couldn't place. Aisha had heard the song a million times before, but she was never sure which singer it was. Brandy, Monica, Aaliyah, or perhaps some combination. She got them all confused. "Way to be in tune with our generation," Nina was always teasing.

As Aisha watched Kendra fold the napkins with careless abandon, all the while singing along to the mindless tune, she felt her rage return once again. How dare Kendra look so happy? It had only been a day ago that she and Kendra had sat down and had a heart-to-heart. Kendra had told her about Carina; she knew how upset Aisha was. She knew what Christopher had done. Yet here she was, humming along merrily to America's Top 40. *She should be worried about me,*

Aisha thought. *She should be worried about her brother. And what I'm going to do to him.*

"Eesh, hey!" Kendra said cheerily when she finally looked up. Aisha held up her hand and gave a little wave. "Your mom said you should start on the laundry—the tablecloths need to be done, and your hamper's full."

"I'll get to that later," Aisha said, her tone purposefully rigid. She watched as Kendra's posture stiffened, her hands letting go of the napkin she'd been folding. "Right now we have to talk," Aisha said adamantly.

"I thought we talked yesterday," Kendra responded meekly. "I promise, Eesh, I told you everything I know. Really."

"I believe you," Aisha replied, although she wasn't sure she did. Kendra nodded eagerly. "But now," Aisha continued, "you've got to help me."

"Help you? How?" Kendra asked.

"I'm going to find Carina," Aisha said. It was funny. She hadn't even known that was what she was going to do until she'd said it.

"You're gonna what?" Kendra gasped, her hands gripping the edge of an unfolded napkin.

"I don't have time to repeat myself," Aisha stated. She knew she sounded like a kindergarten teacher, but she didn't care.

"Aisha," Kendra cried imploringly, "you can't. Christopher will go crazy. You should have seen him yesterday after you told him you didn't want to see him anymore. He went nuts! He's my brother, and I've never seen him like that. He was almost violent!"

"Frankly, Kendra," Aisha answered, her words measured and clipped, "I don't care what Christopher does. I'm doing this for me."

"Eesh!" Kendra cried. "Please give Christopher one

more chance. Please! He can't live without you. It's like that song that was just on the radio. Your love goes 'on and on and on.'"

"Spare me." Aisha groaned.

"Don't break off the engagement with him," Kendra pleaded, standing up. She looked small and fragile all of a sudden. "The ring! He spent so much money on it."

"That's the last thing I care about," Aisha responded icily, looking down at the silver band around her ring finger. "If this ring means anything more than just a call to the Home Shopping Network, then he ought to be able to tell me the truth. But since he won't, I'm going to have to do a little detective work. I'll find out the truth—with or without him."

"Well, what is it you want me to do?" Kendra asked. "I can't go with you—your mom needs me."

"I don't want you to go with me," Aisha snapped. "I just need you to cover for me."

"Cover for you how?" Kendra asked.

"I'll tell you later," Aisha said brusquely. "After I do my chores." She turned her back to Kendra and marched out of the kitchen. She grabbed her book bag off the front-room couch and walked with determination toward her room.

Doing her laundry was now a necessity. She was going to need clean clothes for what she was about to do.

Steam clung to the bathroom tiles, and the medicinal scent of dandruff shampoo hung in the air as Jake dried his body with a clean white terry cloth towel. He wiped the cloudy mirror with the palm of his hand so he could get a closer look at his face. Should he shave? He felt the bristles on his chin. Not too bad. He could last another day. Anyway, Kate was waiting for him down-stairs.

Jake put on his blue-and-green-plaid robe. He was pleased to notice that either he'd gotten bigger or the robe had shrunk because it was tight around the chest and arms. Jake flexed his biceps. "You monsters might be getting too big for your own good," he said. Jake laughed at his own vanity. If only girls knew how ridiculous guys could be sometimes. It was funny to think about it.

Jake tramped down the stairs, the Coolio song still going through his mind. It was kind of weird that Kate had just shown up without calling, but he was happy to have her there. Despite everything they'd been through during their short relationship—her mother's med-dling, Kate's need to go on medication, all Lara McAvoy's attempts to break them up—he was still into Kate. Very into Kate. There was something basic and real about the way they connected. Something he couldn't put into words. Somehow he and Kate as a couple just made sense.

Jake opened the door to the garage. Now that Kate was here, he'd ask her to stay for dinner. They could make pasta and watch television, and then he'd walk her back home to the Cabrals' house, taking the long route along the rocky beaches. . . .

But when Jake entered the room and saw Kate slumped over on the workout bench with her head in her hands, her body aquiver with every muffled sob, he put away any thoughts of having a normal evening.

Kate was in one of her moods.

BENJAMIN

Lies

I don't lie to anyone as much as I lie
to myself.

Every day. I get up in the morning,
look out the window, and think
about how promising the day ahead
looks. I think about how clear and
bright and crisp the outside world is.
I think about how glad I am that I
can see.

And I am. I am glad.

There's only one problem. Sight is a
relative thing. I can see compared to
a blind person. Compared to how I
used to be, I practically have X-ray
vision.

But compared to a normal sighted
person . . . well. That's a different
story.

I just don't want anyone to stand in
my way—I don't want anyone to tell
me that I can't do things because my
vision isn't perfect. So I don't have
twenty-twenty sight—who cares? I
don't want to miss out on anything
anymore. I'm tired of that.

That's why I don't want anyone to

know about—my problem. So don't tell me that I'm lying to myself.

I'll handle it.

Just like I've always handled it.

Seven

"Apparently, Nina, the light of day is not your friend."
Claire grimaced as she ladled a scoop of mashed potatoes onto her plate and inspected her sister's dinner attire:
an oversize football jersey that said Grrrls 'R' Us on the
front and a pair of tattered gray sweatpants. Lately Nina
had been wearing that shirt to sleep almost every night of
the week. The fact that she still had it on was indicative
of one thing: Nina hadn't left her bedroom all day.

"I got up today," Nina shot back defensively.

"The remote control need new batteries or something?" Claire taunted.

Nina cast her a vicious look. "Zoey came over," she
grumbled. "So you could say I spent some of the day
entertaining a friend."

"Hmmmpf," Claire grunted.

"You do know what a 'friend' is, don't you, Claire?"
Nina snapped. "I know you don't have many, but . . ."

Claire didn't have a chance to formulate a retort,
thanks to her dad's interruption. "That's enough,
girls!" Burke Geiger bellowed. "Really. You'd think
you two were still in grade school, the way you gripe at
each other!"

"Sorry, Dad," Nina mumbled.

"Yeah, I apologize, Dad," Claire followed.

"You're lucky your stepmother is off at her oil-painting class and not here," Burke barked. "She wouldn't tolerate any of this yammering."

No one said anything. Claire looked at Nina, who shot her a conspiratorial roll of the eyes. Claire knew that Nina was thinking the same thing she was: *As if*. The idea that Sarah Mendel's opinions had any bearing on either of the two sisters was preposterous. But they could let their dad have his fantasies. They didn't hurt anyone.

"Well, now that we've established that my youngest did a whole lot of nothing today," Burke said, placing his fork on his plate so he could reach over and give Nina an affectionate rub on the head, "what about you, Claire? What did you do today?"

"Yeah, Claire," Nina said, "aside from your raid on my closet, what did you do today?"

There was a lump of mashed potatoes caught in Claire's throat. She swallowed hard and thought about the question. What had she done today? The ironic truth was she hadn't done much more than Nina had. After she'd put her ensemble together, she hadn't really left her room, either. She'd taken more than a few much needed naps to make up for her night of insomnia, and when she had left the confines of her bedroom, it was only to retrieve a sewing kit from the supply drawer in the kitchen. She'd made a few lame attempts at mending her clothes; unfortunately she hadn't had much luck with her handiwork. What was she going to do? Build an entirely new wardrobe? It was a good thing she was going to need stuff for college. It gave her an excuse to hit the mall, courtesy of Burke Geiger's credit card. And she wouldn't have to tell him the real reason she was going shopping.

"Uh, I started going through my clothes and stuff," Claire finally answered. "You know, I need to start

73

thinking about what I'm going to take with me to college."

"Good thinking, honey," Burke intoned. "You can never be too prepared." Claire looked up at her father's beaming face and felt a wave of guilt. What if her stalker tried to hurt him? She'd never be able to live with herself. *I should tell him,* she thought decisively. *I should tell him right now.*

"Another excellent meal!" Burke exclaimed when Janelle walked into the room.

"It's not finished yet," Janelle replied. "I made the apple crumble you like so much." She removed a couple of empty platters from the table and walked back into the kitchen.

"It's a good thing your stepmother isn't here," Burke whispered to the girls. "You know how she feels about me and sweets."

"Your belly's cute, Dad," Nina complimented.

"Well, I'm not sure if Sarah feels the same way." Burke chuckled. "But I've had a hard day at work. The way I see it, I deserve a little of Janelle's apple crumble."

I can't ruin his dessert, Claire thought. *It's the only bright spot in his day. He doesn't need more things to worry about. Besides—how can he help me? What's he going to do?*

Janelle reappeared with the apple crumble in one hand and a pile of mail in the other.

"Ah, Janelle, I forgot about the mail," Burke joked. "What goes better with apple crumble than a juicy pile of bills?"

Janelle placed the bulk of the mail in front of Mr. Geiger. Then she circled the table. "This came for you, Claire," she said, winking. "Looks like it's from a secret admirer," she said softly so only Claire could hear.

Claire held the thick off-white envelope in her hand. *Oh, God, don't be from* him, she thought. She caressed the envelope with her fingers. In thick black ink was calligraphed Claire Geiger. Underneath, her address was etched in a smaller script. *Maybe it's an invitation,* Claire reasoned with herself. *Or maybe it's a note from Aaron.* Claire noticed that there was no postmark on the envelope, no stamp. The note had been hand delivered. *Maybe Aaron was being extra romantic and he arranged for someone to hand deliver this to me,* Claire thought as she delicately ripped open the envelope. Inside was a single note card with nothing on it. *Weird,* Claire thought. But then she turned it over. On the other side of the card, in the same script, a poem was written: *Go outside, and then you'll see/a present on the porch to you from me.*

Aaron wouldn't have written anything so creepy. And he'd never sent her anything without signing it. Claire knew in her heart who the letter was from.

"What have you got there?" Burke inquired warmly. His mouth was full of apple crumble, and he grabbed the cup of coffee Janelle had just poured to wash it down.

"N-N-Nothing," Claire stammered. "Just something from MIT. About housing. Nothing important."

"Found out who your roommate's going to be next year?" Burke asked, shoveling another generous bite into his mouth.

"No," Claire said in a voice that made it clear the subject was closed. She didn't want her father to get suspicious, but college roommates were the last thing she wanted to discuss.

"Why aren't you eating your crumble?" Nina asked, reaching across the table to stick her fork in Claire's untouched dessert.

"I'm not hungry," Claire replied, trying to keep her

voice steady. "Uh, in fact, I think I may have eaten too many mashed potatoes or something. I feel kind of sick." Claire stood up. "I think I'm going to go get some air. Do you mind, Dad?" she asked.

Burke Geiger shook his head. His mouth was too full for him to voice any protest.

Claire pushed her dessert plate toward Nina. She clutched the letter and walked quickly outside to the porch.

Her stomach was killing her.

Benjamin didn't feel like eating much. That was because every time he tried to swallow, a different part of his body ached. It was as if each time he put the fork to his lips, he pulled another muscle.

"Surfing get the better of you, son?" his dad had asked when he'd gotten home from the restaurant. "No," Benjamin had lied. "I'm just tired." Benjamin didn't want to tell his parents about the morning's accident and how Bob had practically saved his life, pulling him out of the ocean. Not only would it completely freak them out but it would also prove their suspicions right: Ever since Benjamin had gotten back his sight, his parents had been begging him to "take it easy," to go for regular checkups at the eye doctor. He hadn't listened to them.

As he sat upright in his chair—every muscle feeling the morning's wipeout, his temples aching with every bite of food—he wondered if perhaps they were right.

"For someone who spends so much time in the sun, you certainly look pale," Mrs. Passmore said. Benjamin's mother had been voicing her concern sporadically throughout the day. "You don't look yourself." "Are you sure you're not feeling under the weather?" "Honey, maybe you should take a nap."

"I'm not tan because I wear a lot of sunscreen," Benjamin offered. "Which is the healthy thing to do," he added. Benjamin peered up at his mother. Was she buying his story? She still looked upset. He was relieved to have his dad step in.

"Speaking of news," Mr. Passmore interrupted. "How was our junior journalist's first day home?"

Benjamin was relieved. Now the conversation's focus was on Zoey. And he was going to try to keep it there.

"It was okay," Zoey replied chirpily. Benjamin watched as she twirled a piece of linguine around her fork. Or was that fettuccine? Benjamin prided himself on being quite the gourmand. So why couldn't he tell the difference between the two?

"Okay!" his father joked. "That doesn't seem like a word a journalist would choose. Not very descriptive at all."

"Sorry, Dad," Zoey said, flashing Benjamin her "parents can be so tiresome" look (or was that her "lovable old Dad" look? Benjamin was having a difficult time distinguishing between them). "I guess you could say my day was a number of things. It started out really nice, but then it took a turn for the weird."

"How so, honey?" Mrs. Passmore asked. Benjamin had never appreciated Zoey's presence more. Not only did she have their dad's attention, but now she had their mom's. *Maybe Mom won't keep staring at my full plate,* Benjamin thought. He would have breathed a sigh of relief if he didn't think it would fill his entire body with a searing pain. Damn that surfing accident.

"Oh, well, I don't know," Zoey was saying. "I guess it just takes a bit of time to get used to being back." Her parents nodded, apparently satisfied. Zoey turned to Benjamin. "I did see Nina today," she said pointedly.

What am I supposed to say to that? Benjamin

thought angrily. "Oh, yeah," he mumbled nonchalantly. "How's Nin?"

"I don't know," Zoey answered. "I think she's upset about stuff."

Benjamin could feel the hair on the back of his neck bristle. Nina upset? The last time he'd seen her, she'd seemed perfectly content. Preoccupied but pretty happy. He'd had the definite feeling that she was over him, which made sense, considering how over her he was. So what if he'd thought about her this morning? It was just a smell that had triggered it. Otherwise he had moved totally beyond her. Really, he had.

"Benjamin," Zoey cried. She sounded exasperated. "I think Nina's upset over *you*. She didn't leave her room all day. She just sat there, watching television. She didn't say anything, but I could tell—she's heartbroken!"

How like his sister to get all melodramatic. "I'm sure she's fine," Benjamin said. "Really, Zo."

"I've always liked Nina," Mr. Passmore said, although no one had asked him.

"Same here," Mrs. Passmore agreed. She stood up and began to collect the dirty dishes. When she stopped at Benjamin's place, she said, "Well, I don't know if you should have dessert, considering that you barely ate anything."

Does she think I'm twelve years old? Benjamin wondered somewhat testily. He turned to Zoey. "Look, I've always liked Nina, too. It's not that I don't like her, it's just that I can't be her boyfriend right now."

Zoey's mouth was a tight line. "It's just that you don't want to be her boyfriend right now even though she needs you," she countered.

"Whatever," Benjamin growled, but he thought: *What do you know about what I want?*

Eight

The Front Porch,
the Geiger House

Claire held the shoe-box-size package in her hands. It was neatly wrapped in brown paper, and when Claire shook it, she could hear that it contained something small and solid. "Oh, God, what if it's a bomb?" she wondered to herself. Her head filled with images of cartoon-style violence: a huge explosion, a big blam, her long black hair sticking up on end, her face covered with dark ashy smudges, the Geiger porch half decimated.

Claire shook the package again. Come to think of it, if this was a bomb, shaking it was probably a bad idea.

Second only to opening it.

The Front Steps,
the Passmore House

And on to phase two, Lara thought. On the way back from the docks she'd decided that she needed to come up with a proper strategy to break up Zoey and Lucas. She'd come to the conclusion that concentrating on Lucas's actions (rather than Zoey's) was the ticket to success. There was something about his face this morning—something that made her suspicious. He'd seemed a little uncomfortable. *Perhaps he's already done something he's sorry for,* Lara thought. Lara was always somewhat psychically in tune to people—and she was getting a weird reading on Lucas. If she could discover something about him that Zoey didn't know, a secret he was keeping from her, that would be all she needed to majorly kick her plan into motion. It didn't have to be anything major. Lara could make something major out of something minor. Or out of nothing at all, for that matter.

"Pasta-making classes don't start for a few days, you know." Lara turned her head to see her half brother, Benjamin, calling to her from the kitchen window.

"I know!" Lara smiled, remembering that her dad had offered to give her and Benjamin some cooking classes at the restaurant. "I'm just dropping by to say hey," she explained.

"Well, you actually just missed the Passmore fettuccine special," Benjamin replied.

"No fair getting a head start on those classes," Lara mocked. He grinned. Lara loved her relationship with her half brother. He was so good-natured and genuine. And unlike his sister, he definitely wasn't boring. He actually appreciated art (hers in particular) and was into talking about things other than himself and his small circle of friends. *It's easy to see who got all the good genes in the Passmore family,* Lara thought spitefully.

"What I really need is a walk," Benjamin called out the window. "Wanna come?"

Lara didn't really mind putting aside her plan to go inside and see if Zoey and Lucas were there in favor of hanging out with Benjamin. Besides, any excuses she offered would probably make him suspicious.

"Okay," she agreed. There would always be time to wreak havoc later.

The Side Porch,
the Gray Inn

Aisha couldn't stop pacing. Her parents had said they'd come outside after dinner. Where were they? If she was going to lie to them, she wanted to get it over with fast. Aisha had considered telling them the truth: that she was taking a little solo sojourn in search of Christopher's ex-wife. "It won't take that long. I can't imagine I'd have that much to say to a drug addict," she'd imagined herself saying.

Somehow telling them the whole story seemed like a bad idea. She suspected it would be too much of an ordeal.

She'd had enough of that.

The Deck,
the Cabral House

Lucas stood on the deck of his house and stared out into the evening. He wondered briefly how much of his life he'd spent standing in this exact same spot. It provided him the perfect view of the Passmore house; specifically, of Zoey's room. Sometimes the two of them would make signs to each other out the windows—Lucas would look for Zoey's lights to turn on in the morning, to go out at night. Remembering those times, Lucas felt momentarily at peace. *I love Zoey,* Lucas thought, *more than anything or anyone. I always have.*

Then what was the explanation for his behavior earlier? Lucas had acted like such a jerk this morning; he'd felt terrible about it all day.

Lucas wasn't one to lapse into amateur psychology, but he was pretty sure he could successfully analyze the reasons for his jerkiness.

Well, I'm not going to be a jerk tonight, Lucas promised himself. He glanced at his digital watch. He'd better go. Zoey and he were going to the movies, and they needed to catch the next ferry if they were going to make it.

The Terrace, the Passmore House

Zoey stepped outside for a second. She wanted to test the weather. *Sweater or jacket?* she wondered as she exposed her bare arm to the evening breeze. She was wearing a lavender cotton skirt with a short-sleeved white button-down shirt. A windbreaker would definitely ruin the look, she decided. Instead she opted for her white cardigan sweater with antique buttons. She'd probably be cold on the ferry, but she'd be fine once they got to the movie theater. She peered down at the front walkway toward the Cabrals' house to see if Lucas was on his way. She didn't see him coming, but she did see something else: Lara and Benjamin ambling toward the house. They looked relaxed, almost giddy in each other's presence.

Zoey groaned involuntarily.

Thank God I'm getting out of here.

The Side Porch,
the Gray Inn

"Mom and Dad, I know it's short notice, but I'm thinking I should go to Princeton for a couple of days. You know, just check out the housing situation."

Aisha watched as her parents mulled over what she'd just said. Her mom had a pursed look on her face, and her dad looked pensive.

She could tell she had a long and unwieldy conversation ahead of her: her parents hashing it out as they weighed the pros and cons, came up with alternate suggestions, discussed safety and money issues.

But Aisha was ready. She was ready for anything.

The Front Porch,
the Geiger House

Claire wished she hadn't opened the box. If only she could turn back time, she'd have left the box in its wrapping and thrown it in the garbage. Because underneath the two layers of protective fabric (which she recognized as the shredded remains of her green gown) lay a mouse that smelled distinctly dead.

When she'd realized what the box contained, Claire had instinctively dropped it with a startled shriek. When she'd done that, a note had fallen out.

This mouse is dead. All things die, Claire.

Nine

When Lara and Benjamin entered the Passmores' house after their walk, Mr. and Mrs. Passmore were sitting at the kitchen table, forks poised above a tin pan brimming with the remains of a creamy-looking confection.

"You're just in time for leftover dessert, kids," Mr. Passmore boomed. "Pull up a seat."

"Don't mind if I do," Benjamin answered. Lara didn't respond.

She didn't want to say anything, but the dessert—whatever it was—didn't look too appetizing. And the whole communal thing kind of made Lara sick. Maybe she'd actually been affected by the sterile conditions at the rehab center or something. All Lara knew was that as hungry as she was—she hadn't eaten all day—she wasn't too eager to engage in the sugar smorgasbord. Even if all the participating members were "family."

Which is what the Passmores were. Whether they wanted to be or not.

Lara politely refused the dessert. "Well, then, have you come to enjoy our company? Or have you come to finish the great masterpiece?" Mr. Passmore asked. He was referring to the painting of him Lara had started the last time she was over.

"If you have time, I'd love to do a few strokes," Lara answered.

"Of course I have the time," Mr. Passmore said. "Who wouldn't have time to pose for one of the next great artists of this century?"

Lara blushed. She knew her father was trying to be nice, but she couldn't help feeling that sometimes he tried to compensate for his absence during the first eighteen years of her life with compliments.

Lara hadn't asked Benjamin if Zoey was home; she'd just assumed that she and Lucas would be there. She tried to hide her disappointment when she didn't see the two anywhere. Where were they, anyway?

Mrs. Passmore answered her unasked question. "I hope Zoey's not mad that we didn't save any cake for her, but I'm sure she and Lucas got some snacks at the movies."

The movies. So that's where the dynamic duo were. *How precious,* Lara thought.

"So, Lara, you ready for me to pose?" Mr. Passmore inquired as he stood up from the table, his crumb-covered plate in hand. "I think I know exactly where we'll put the great work," he joked, pointing to an empty spot above the knickknack-covered mantelpiece in the living room.

Lara tried to conjure up a smile. The idea of working on the portrait wasn't as appealing as it had been, now that she knew Lucas and Zoey weren't around. But the movies couldn't last forever. Maybe Lucas would come back with Zoey, and Lara could scrutinize the couple in all their postcinematic bliss.

Benjamin sidled up to her. "I think you've really tapped into Dad's vanity," Benjamin whispered in her ear. The two of them watched as their father emerged from the bottom-floor bathroom, his face freshly scrubbed, his hair combed back neatly. He took a seat on a kitchen chair.

"Okay, Lara, as the saying goes . . . I'm ready for my close-up!" Mr. Passmore sat back and adapted a regal pose. He reminded Lara of a peacock, with his chest puffed out. She couldn't hide a smile, although she tried.

Benjamin gave Lara's short-cropped hair a playful tug. "Looks like you've got a long night ahead of you," he quipped.

You don't know the half of it, Lara mused.

Considering how badly their morning interaction had gone, Zoey couldn't believe how easy it was to be with Lucas now. For the first time in the history of their relationship, Lucas hadn't grumbled when Zoey had chosen to see a romantic comedy over an action flick, and he'd kept her from getting chilly in the air-conditioned theater by wrapping an arm around her.

Lucas's behavior was such a departure from his morning mood that Zoey almost wanted to ask him whether she had said something wrong this morning or whether she had said something right this evening. But she didn't. *Why ruin a good thing?* she asked herself. *Anyway, you promised yourself there wouldn't be any heavy talk. Just you and Lucas having a good time.*

Zoey's eyes still burned from having sat too close to the movie screen, and as they headed toward the food court the sight of all the neon signs flashing in unison—Sushi, Pizza, California Cuisine, Cinnamon Buns, Submarine Sandwiches, Coffee—made her feel a bit dizzy. Zoey couldn't decide whether she wanted to eat anymore. She'd had a full dinner, and she and Lucas had split a box of Milk Duds at the movies.

Maybe she'd just have a cappuccino at the new espresso place.

"You want to go sit somewhere?" she asked Lucas, giving his hand a little squeeze.

"Okay," he answered. His arm was slung over her shoulder as they walked, and he moved his hand upward to squeeze the back of her neck affectionately. Zoey could still feel his touch after he moved his hand away.

"Coffee?" Zoey asked.

Lucas shook his head. "No caffeine late at night for me," he said. "I need to sleep. Considering I have to be up in a few hours."

Zoey felt inconsiderate for having asked. "Frozen yogurt?" she said.

Zoey took Lucas's silence as a yes, and she led them toward the yogurt stand. They ordered banana-and-chocolate combination swirls with rainbow sprinkles and went to find seats at the orange plastic tables near the Hamburger Stand. They were Zoey's favorite seats in the food court because they offered both privacy and a place to people watch.

Lucas used one hand to dole yogurt into his mouth with a plastic spoon while he placed the other hand on Zoey's thigh. He'd positioned their seats as close together as possible. Having him so near made Zoey feel warm all over—even as the cold yogurt was gliding down her throat.

Between bites Lucas would turn to Zoey and give her quick kisses on the cheek. His lips felt cold and sticky, but she didn't mind. It was such a relief to have the old Lucas back. *What was I so worried about this morning?* she wondered. *He was just in a bad mood.*

Zoey told him about D.C.—about how the city smelled in the sweltering heat; about her nightmarish roommate, MaryBeth; about how she'd thought about him constantly.

Zoey was in the middle of a ridiculous anecdote involving MaryBeth, a lost retainer, and the youth hostel cafeteria when she saw Lucas's face drop.

Suddenly he was no longer laughing or smiling. Had she said something wrong?

"Lucas, are you okay?" she asked, recalling how defensive he'd gotten earlier when all she'd asked him was how he was.

"Yeah," he answered, but the tone of his voice made it difficult for Zoey to believe him. He'd removed his hand from her thigh and moved his gaze downward so that he was staring at his black low-top sneakers as they nervously tapped the glossy white Formica floor.

"Lucas, what's wrong?" Zoey wanted to know. "Did I say something wrong?" She reached for his hand.

Zoey's eyes were boring into Lucas's face as she tried to make sense of what she saw there. Finally she followed his gaze a few tables down.

Sitting at another orange plastic table, their chairs surrounded by shopping bags, were Claire and Nina Geiger.

"Oh, my God, I didn't know Nina and Claire were coming to the mall!" Zoey exclaimed happily when she finally turned to see them.

"Why would they be here?" Lucas's tone sounded almost accusatory.

Zoey looked confused. Was this the source of his angst? Claire and Nina? Here Zoey had thought she'd triggered some thought about his dead father, and the only reason he was upset was that her friends were nearby. *Has Lucas gotten this antisocial?* Zoey wondered. She was at a loss about what to do. Lucas was now clutching her hand again, this time in a quick-let's-head-for-cover kind of way, but Zoey couldn't just ignore her best friend—even if she could ignore Claire. Anyway, what better time to set Operation Friendship into action?

"Be nice to Nina," Zoey whispered to Lucas as she dragged him by the elbow to the Geigers' table. He was clutching his melted yogurt. He emitted a reluctant grunt. "You know, she's pretty broken up about Benjamin," Zoey explained. "I'm so glad she's out and about. Maybe our talk earlier helped her."

"You and Nina talked earlier?" Lucas asked.

"Um, Lucas," Zoey said, a line appearing between her eyebrows, "I talk to Nina fairly often. Look, we'll just go over for a second," she promised. She led him by the hand to the Geigers' table. "Hey!" she said, smiling. "What are you guys doing here?"

"Um, shopping?" Claire replied sarcastically, as if Zoey had asked the stupidest question on earth.

Sometimes Claire could be so rude, Zoey thought. *I guess she's having an off day. At least that would explain her outfit.* "Isn't that Nina's skirt?" Zoey asked.

Claire ignored her.

"Personally, I'm trying to figure out what this wrap craze is all about. I mean, it's supposed to be the latest thing, but I don't get what all the hoopla is about—it just seems like a mess to me," Nina said, skipping over a greeting. Zoey couldn't help but notice that her best friend was talking very fast. It was practically gibberish that was coming out of her cherry-red-painted lips. "I mean, hello, how do you eat this thing?" she asked, jabbing the mess of rice, vegetables, and pita bread with her pinkie finger. "It's like there are too many ingredients or something; is this cilantro or is it parsley, who can tell, and with the beans and the rice and the orange flecks of—omigod—is that *carrot?* I think it *is*," she continued, pulling a unrecognizable orangish clump from the mush.

"Gee, Nina, I think you might be right," Zoey replied. Why was Nina behaving so oddly? Had too much TV affected her brain?

There was an awkward silence during which no one really said anything. Zoey felt like she was in the twilight zone or something. Lucas was acting sullen, Claire's eyes kept darting around like she was looking for someone, and Nina seemed unable to concentrate on anything other than the blob of food in her hand.

Maybe this isn't the time to launch Operation Friendship, Zoey thought. Then again, she didn't know when the next time she'd get Lucas and Nina in the same room would be. She decided to take a stab at it. "Hey, you know, Nina, I have good news for you."

Nina looked up expectantly from her messy plate. "Yeah?" she said.

"Lucas is gonna be hanging out on the island next year!" she said cheerily. "You guys can hang out."

Silence.

"Oh, uh, Zo, uh, I—I know. I mean, that's great. That is, it's kind of not so great for you, Lucas," Nina finally stumbled. "But I'll be glad to have some company."

Lucas didn't respond. But his lips were pursed tightly, and he was looking at the floor again.

As she and Lucas walked back toward the ferry Zoey felt she'd made a massive mistake. Lucas obviously thought what she'd said about staying home on the island was insensitive when all she'd been trying to do was put a positive spin on everything. "Positive spin" was a term she'd learned at the journalism con-

90.

vention. It meant that she was trying to put the bad news in the best-possible light.

Well, it hadn't worked with Lucas.

The rift between them seemed to have returned. Zoey felt incredibly cold as she stepped onto the ferry. She hugged herself to keep warm, hoping Lucas would take the hint and wrap his arms around her. He didn't.

I should have worn my windbreaker, she thought with a sigh.

By the time Zoey got home, Lara was beyond sick of painting. She'd been so fixated on her stepsister's impending return, she hadn't been able to focus on the portrait. As a result Mr. Passmore's nose looked like a frying pan had hit it or something. Lara couldn't figure out what she'd done wrong, but it was a pretty major flaw.

"Have a good time, honey?" Mr. Passmore called when he heard the front door slam.

"Yes, Dad," came Zoey's voice from the other room. Lara listened for Lucas's footsteps. She was hoping that the two of them would go down to the family room so that she could join them. But Zoey hadn't even brought Lucas home with her!

Lara's night was a total bust, except for the walk with Benjamin. Not only had she messed up her painting, but she'd gotten nowhere with her scheme.

But she wasn't giving up.

I can't believe I messed up again, Zoey thought as she lay in bed. She wanted to apologize but worried that raising the subject again would only make Lucas angrier.

I'll make it up to him tomorrow, she told herself.

Ten

Aisha's bags were packed, but she decided she was going to give Christopher one more chance. Not that he deserved it. But she felt she owed it to herself. If she called Christopher and he came clean about Carina, well, she'd save herself a lot of time and effort.

Aisha glanced at the digital clock on the nightstand next to her bed. Ten thirty-five P.M. She tried to imagine what Christopher would be doing right now. He'd probably just come home from work. He'd be lying on the couch and watching the day's sports highlights on the news. There'd be an open bag of chips or popcorn on the coffee table in front of him, and he'd be swigging from a bottle of old-fashioned root beer.

Imagining the scene gave Aisha a momentary pang. Was it just a week ago that she'd been an integral part of that scenario? She should be sitting on the couch with an old wool army blanket over her knees and Christopher's head in her lap, complaining about how boring the basketball highlights were and tickling him under his chin so that he wouldn't fall asleep because he had to walk her home before midnight.

Aisha let out a long sigh. Those times seemed so far

away—everything was so different now. Would she ever do those things again?

Aisha held a portable phone in one hand and a black-and-white composition book in the other. She had been using the book for her astronomy lab calculations, but she'd spent the last few hours transforming it into a makeshift research journal/travelogue. Aisha had filled the pages with notes and lists. She'd methodically transcribed all the bits and pieces of information that Kendra had given her. She'd composed lists of things to do, questions to ask, goals to meet. All involving Carina Connelly.

Aisha turned the page to the first list she'd written.

What to Ask Christopher When You Call Him

1. Why did you lie about Carina?
2. Why do you value protecting her over being honest with me?
3. Is it because you're still in love with her?
4. Were you ever going to tell me about her?
5. Did you think I would never find out?
6. What else don't I know?

Aisha was aware that these were some pretty heavy-weight questions, but she didn't care. She needed answers.

Aisha could feel the indignation in her fingertips as she dialed the familiar numbers. She'd just lay it on the line for Christopher. She'd tell him what the deal was going to be: Either he told her the truth, or the engagement was off.

Aisha's face got hotter with every ring. One. Two. Three. Why wasn't Christopher picking up? Four. Five. *If I get the answering machine, I'm just going to hang up,* Aisha decided. *I won't give him time to formulate some pack of lies before he calls me back.*

On the sixth ring Christopher picked up. "Hello?" His voice was groggy and crackly. He was asleep.

There was something startling about the sound of Christopher's sleepy voice. He sounded so sweet and vulnerable, Aisha almost didn't go through with it. She thought about putting the receiver down but stopped herself. *Do what you planned,* her inner voice said. "Hello?" Christopher asked a second time.

"I thought you'd be awake," was all Aisha could think to say.

"Eesh," Christopher moaned. Aisha could hear the rustle of sheets and blankets. "I have the early shift tomorrow, so I was trying to get a little extra sleep," he explained. "But I'm glad you called. Don't worry about waking me up. . . ."

"I wasn't worried," Aisha snapped, affronted. "I don't care one bit whether I wake you."

Christopher mumbled something unintelligible, and Aisha barreled on. "I'm giving you the chance to tell me about Carina," she stormed. There was silence on the other end of the receiver. She peered down at her list. "Why did you lie about her?"

"Aisha, please listen to me," Christopher cried, his voice cracking. "I can't tell you! You have to trust me."

"That's absurd, Christopher," Aisha scoffed. She tried to keep her voice down. The last thing she needed was to wake up one of her parents or, worse—one of the boarders.

"I can't believe protecting her is more important than being honest with me!" Aisha cupped her hand around the receiver to muffle the shrillness in her voice.

"I didn't say that, Eesh," Christopher replied. He wasn't bending.

Aisha couldn't believe it. She glanced at her list again. At this rate she would get through the questions pretty fast. Of course, she wouldn't have a single answer. "Christopher, I'm giving you one last chance! Or else!"

"Or else what?" Christopher asked.

It took Aisha a minute to get the words out, but finally she did. What choice did she have? "Or else I won't marry you."

Aisha gave Christopher a few seconds to respond, although they felt like an eternity. "I don't know what to say," he said finally.

"Well, I do," Aisha answered icily. She hung up the phone.

She hadn't even made it to question three.

Claire sat on her bed amidst a sea of purchases. *Nothing like a little retail therapy to make a girl forget a dead mouse,* she told herself. She'd totally gone for it at the mall. Four new skirts of varying hem length. Ten new T-shirts (there had been a two-for-one sale at Contempo Casuals). Three new cardigan sweaters in varying shades of blue. Four dresses in floral prints. A couple of pairs of jeans. And a velour A-line miniskirt that Nina had talked her into buying when they were in the skateboard shop.

"How come all the clothes look like they're something I would have worn in fourth grade?" Claire had asked.

"Duh," Nina had retorted in her oh-so-clever way as she held an oversize early-eighties-style Adidas workout suit against her body and observed her reflection in the mirror. "It's retro, Claire. Where have you been all year? Retro's been the rage! In fact, it's already practically over."

Claire had shrugged. "Wasn't it over to begin with?" she'd wanted to ask, but hadn't. She hadn't had the energy to get into some battle over style semantics with Nina. Anyway, Nina's question stuck in her head. Where had she been? Well, she'd been studying, mainly. Working her way toward MIT. There'd been a short period when she'd tried to break up her father's marriage. And then she'd gotten serious with Aaron. There'd been graduation. Aaron's near betrayal. And now this most recent episode had consumed her life. . . .

Claire shook her head as she tried not to think about her stalker or the dead mouse or the letters or anything bad. Instead she turned her mind back to Aaron. An image of her long lost boyfriend—with his chiseled features, his thick dark hair, and his devilish grin—overtook Claire, and she grabbed for the last unopened shopping bag. It was from Victoria's Secret. Nina might have harassed Claire into some unnecessary purchases at the skateboard shop, but Claire had gotten her back by spending more than an ample amount of time perusing the racks of bras and lingerie at the Victoria's Secret store on the second floor of the mall.

"I bet most of these things were made by men," Nina

had grumbled. "Evil men at that," she'd added with a glance at Claire. "Either that or women-hating women named Helga." She'd picked up a red satin bra and inspected all the hooks and wires. "Is this a torture device or a bra?" she'd scoffed.

Claire had done her best to ignore the psychosis that was her sister. Instead she'd moved on to the shelves lined with sleepwear. She'd thought about getting a nightgown, but thumbing the fabric had made her remember the gown she'd tried to wear to sleep last night. It had been one of the first shredded garments she'd discovered. Claire had felt a shiver shoot from the top of her neck down to her spine as she'd stood in front of the store display, remembering her tattered gown. And she'd nearly fainted when the store clerk had approached her from behind. "Can I help you?" the woman had asked. The unexpected voice had scared Claire so badly, she'd been unable to respond. "Interested in some nightgowns?" the woman had persisted. Claire had shaken her head. *"Habla español?"* the woman had asked. Claire had walked away.

Claire had been so creeped out, she'd left the night-gown room and walked to the other side of the store, where the pajamas were kept. There she'd settled on a pair of white satin shorty pajamas with a royal blue trim. They were sexy and girly, but practical all the same. "I didn't know culottes were back in," Nina had jibed as they stood on line for the cash register.

Claire held the Victoria's Secret shopping bag by the handles. She opened it up. Her pajamas were swathed by a layer of pink-flowered tissue paper. *I'll put these on now,* Claire thought. *Maybe they'll inspire me to get a good night's sleep.*

When Claire removed the tissue-paper-covered package from the bag, it fell open to reveal professionally folded pajamas. On top of them lay an off-white envelope.

The same kind as she'd gotten before.

Claire could feel bile fill her throat. He'd gotten into her bag. He'd been following her. He'd been close enough to slip this into her bag. *He'd been right there.*

Claire scoured her brain, trying to remember who— if anyone—had gotten close enough to them. But it was impossible to remember the nameless faces of the teeming crowds that had filled the mall.

Claire spent a good long minute gazing down at the envelope, and she was trembling as she opened it up and removed its contents—a thick off-white note card on which was written:

All this shopping can't stop you from feeling lonely, Claire.

There was no way Claire was going to be able to sleep.

Pajamas or no pajamas.

Eleven

Sean had slept well last night. Exceptionally well. It was a good thing he'd moved from that rat hole of a youth hostel in North Harbor to the bed-and-breakfast place on the island. He grabbed a matchbook off the nighttable next to the bed. The Gray Inn, that was it.

Sean had to admit: The place was a little quaint for his taste. The double bed was covered with a flowered coverlet. The desk was old and wooden and looked like it was straight out of an old-fashioned schoolroom. The soap in the bathroom was lilac scented. And everything was small. The bathtub was small. The television set was small. The pillows, although plentiful, were all small.

Then again, to Sean, everything seemed small. That was because, once upon a time, he'd been very large. "A man of substance," was how his mom used to refer to him. That had been a nice way of saying "fat."

Recently, though, Sean had lost weight. He'd gone on a special high-protein–low-carbohydrate diet, and he'd started running. He'd lost about a hundred pounds. But although he was no longer obese, he still felt like he was. People who thought that eating disorders went away after successful diets were completely wrong.

As thin as he'd become, Sean was as compulsive about food as he'd ever been. If not more so.

Sean opened his duffel bag and pulled out a pair of khaki chinos and a white T-shirt. That was all he usually wore. Style-free and anonymous, all-purpose clothes. He had a busy day today, and these would work just fine.

Sean left the bulk of his belongings—clothes, papers, notebooks—strewn across the room. He folded up his laptop computer (how out of place it looked sitting on the old-fashioned desk!) and headed down for the free breakfast in the inn dining room. A young girl—Sean figured she was probably about sixteen, only a couple of years younger than he—was standing behind a buffet table, pouring hot coffee into china cups.

"Good morning," she chirped. "Coffee?" Sean nodded.

"Okay," the girl said. "And what else would you like? We've got cranberry-orange muffins, cherry Danishes, and low fat pumpkin-spice scones."

Sean bristled when she said "low fat." *She said that just because I'm overweight,* he thought, forgetting that wasn't true anymore. "Uh, don't you have something with protein in it?" Sean asked. "Egg whites? Turkey sausages?"

"The muffins are really filling," the girl responded a little uncomfortably. "And they're unlimited," she stumbled. "I mean, you can have as many as you want."

Sean's face turned hot with embarrassment. *She thinks I'm a huge ugly pig,* he thought angrily.

"Just coffee will be fine," he responded brusquely. He avoided making eye contact with her as she carefully handed him a daintily painted cup and saucer. Balancing the cup in one hand, he used the other to grab a fistful of Equal packets out of a silver bowl.

He turned on the heels of his work boots and looked for a dark table off in the corner.

* * *

"Do not tell me that crank caller is starting before 10 A.M.," Nina grumbled. "Isn't it a little early for psychos?"

Out of the corner of her sleep-filled eye Nina watched her red Elmo phone as it let out a series of high-pitched rings. The local public broadcasting company had recently sent Nina the phone as thanks for her contribution to their telethon (sometimes Dad's credit card came in so handy!).

When—after four rings—no one picked up the phone, Nina decided the duty was hers.

"Yeah," she grumbled, expecting to hear heavy breathing.

"Hey, it's Zoey." Nina shot to attention. Hearing her best friend's voice woke her right up. *Oh, God,* Nina thought, *she's going to ask me why I was so weird at the mall. She's going to accuse me of having been with Lucas. And what will I do? I'll have to tell the truth. . . .*

"Nina, are you there?" Zoey's voice sounded alarmingly officious. *She sounds like she's got something important to tell me,* Nina thought, *and I've got a good guess what it is.*

Nina clutched Elmo tightly and bit her bottom lip in anticipation. "Yeah, Zo," she answered quietly. "I'm here."

"Did Aisha call you?" Zoey asked.

Aisha? What does Aisha have to do with anything? Nina wondered. "What do you mean, did Aisha call me?" she asked.

"Nina!" Zoey exclaimed. "It's not that complicated! What I'm asking you is: Did Aisha call you?"

"N-N-No," Nina stammered, fearing the worst. What if Zoey and Aisha were going to gang up on her together? Zoey had gone crying to Aisha, who'd got-

101

ten appropriately outraged, and the two of them were coming to tell her what a crappy friend she was.

"Well," Zoey said, "she called me. She sounded desperate. She wants us to meet her down at the ferry stop."

"When?" Nina asked. "Why?"

"In ten minutes. I have no idea."

"What do you think the deal is?" Nina asked, unbelievably relieved to discover this wasn't about her and her amoral ways.

"I guess we're about to find out," Zoey answered. Just then Nina's call waiting beeped. "I'll let you get that," Zoey said. "I'll see you in a few minutes." She hung up the phone.

Nina clicked over to the other line. "Hello?" she said.

"Did Zoey call you?" It was Aisha.

Sean walked down along Coast Road. His pace was slow and plodding.

"There's got to be a place around here that serves something I can eat. Something on my diet. If I eat a cranberry-orange muffin, I'll be hungry all day. Just one of those, and I'll be out of control. Oh, she tried to tempt me. The pretty girl wanted me to eat the muffin, but I wouldn't do it—no, I wouldn't fall for her trick because I'm too smart. Did she think I would fall for that?"

The road was deserted, so there was no one to answer Sean's questions or respond to his complaints. He was okay with that, though.

He was used to talking into a void.

"Quick, fast, and right away," were Aisha's final words before she'd hung up the phone.

Nina had no idea what was going on, but she was

pretty desperate to find out. She threw on an old polo shirt of her dad's and a pair of polyester pants that were frayed along the cuffs. When she'd picked them up at a secondhand store a few weeks ago, they'd been in mint condition. Unfortunately something funny had happened to them in the wash. Not only had they begun unraveling but they'd also gone from being salmon colored to bubble gum pink.

"What a shock to see you up at this hour," her father chimed as she came tumbling down the stairs. She nearly tripped on the lace of her right high-top.

"Emergency," Nina mumbled, bending down to tie her sneaker. The laces had rainbows on them, but Nina had dragged them through the mud so much, they were basically black.

"Oh, dear," was all Burke Geiger could say. "I hope it's nothing serious." He furrowed his brow.

Nina didn't say anything.

"Don't you think you should brush your hair before you go out?" That was Sarah Mendel speaking. Nina hadn't seen her standing outside the doorway to the kitchen, but there she was in all her bath-robed, hair-curlered glory, a low fat yogurt in one hand, a bottle of mineral water in the other.

"No time," Nina answered. She scooted into the kitchen, grabbed a box of Cap'n Crunch's Crunch Berries off the counter, and headed for the front door.

"Don't you want to eat those before you go?" she heard Sarah call out. "You know, most people have milk with their cereal! And they use a bowl and a spoon!"

But Nina was already halfway down the block.

"I would like an egg white omelette cooked in very little butter, with onions and bell peppers inside. Please don't sauté the vegetables; I want them raw. I would also like a side of seven-grain toast if you have it, wheat is fine if you don't, and I want it dry with some margarine on the side. And I would like to substitute a green salad for the home fries. And some coffee—with skim milk," Sean barked.

"Will that be all?" the waiter asked.

He's got to be joking, Sean thought incredulously, giving the waiter the once-over. The guy looked like a stand-up kind of guy—he had a nice face. *But he shouldn't be making fun of me,* Sean thought angrily. *I mean, this guy works in a dive called Burger Heaven, and he's got the nerve to ask me: 'Will that be all?' If he's not careful, I'll teach him how to be nice.*

"Yes, that will be all," Sean responded, his voice dripping with sarcasm. The waiter walked away, seemingly nonplussed. He returned momentarily with Sean's coffee.

"You want some sugar?" he asked.

"Equal will be fine . . . Jake," Sean replied, reading the waiter's name tag.

"Here you go, then," Jake replied, putting some sweeteners of various kinds in front of Sean's place and walking toward the grill. Sean turned his head and watched as Jake gave the order to the cook. "No, just the whites; no yolks," he heard him say.

Sean bided his time, reading the *Chatham Island Gazette,* a local freebie magazine he'd stolen from the magazine rack at the Gray Inn. He opened it up to the center spread. The headline read, Islanders Graduate! Chatham Island Student Wins Coveted Valedictorian Spot! Underneath was a picture of five students standing together, all of whom had won different awards.

Sean studied the picture. When he looked up, Jake was standing above him, two plates of food in his hands. "Here you go," Jake offered.

Sean looked at Jake, then he looked at the picture, then he looked at Jake. His waiter had apparently been awarded Athlete of the Year.

"Yeah, that's me," Jake answered when Sean said he recognized him. He looked sort of embarrassed.

"And you know that girl standing next to you?" Sean asked.

"Uh-huh," Jake responded. "That's Claire Geiger. Total babe, huh?"

Sean nodded as he stabbed the omelette with his fork. "Yeah," he intoned, taking his first mouthful. "Total babe."

"Oh, my God, Eesh, don't tell me you're pulling a me!" Nina cried when she saw Aisha sitting on a bench outside the ferry dock. There was a duffel bag by her feet, and she was reading a green tourist's guidebook to Boston.

The walk from her house to the ferry dock had knocked the wind out of Nina, and she happily collapsed next to Aisha. She put her hand in the box of cereal and shoved a handful into her mouth.

"Thanks for getting here so quickly," Aisha said.

"No problemo," Nina mumbled between crunches. "But Eesh," she implored once she'd chewed and swallowed. "What's going on?"

"Yeah, what is going on?" Nina looked up to see that Zoey had arrived. She was wearing a blue spandex crop top, black leggings, and white running shoes and was jogging in place. Sometimes it was hard to have a best friend who looked like Zoey Passmore. She was near perfect looking. Not in the way that Claire was beautiful—cold and unassuming—rather, Zoey was warm and sweet looking. And she had an amazing body. *Lucas must love how good she looks,* Nina thought longingly as she inspected Zoey's narrow waist and long legs. She looked down at the Cap'n Crunch's Crunch Berries. They didn't taste so good all of a sudden.

"And so," Aisha was relaying, "I just feel like I have to go. I have to see who this woman is. I can't marry Christopher without knowing what Carina Connelly is all about."

"Do you have enough money?" Zoey asked.

"How long are you going to be gone?" Nina asked.

The two proceeded to pummel Aisha with questions. When the ferry bell rang, they were still less than satisfied. "But Eesh, what if she really is a drug addict?" Zoey was asking. "Please be careful!" she warned.

"Yeah," Nina agreed. "Next thing you know, you'll be going to raves with Christopher's ex!"

Aisha laughed and gave Nina and Zoey a quick hug each. Nina was pretty certain she could feel her friend trembling.

Or was that her? Suddenly Nina was feeling very nervous about being alone with Zoey.

"You must be new around here," Jake said.

Sean nodded. His mouth was full of eggs and toast.

"You here visiting friends or something?" Jake asked.

"You could kind of say that," Sean said noncommittally.

Jake looked at him oddly, then gave him a little wink. "Oh, I get it!" he declared all of a sudden. "You're here to see a girl."

Sean felt his face flush. He had to admit he liked the way that sounded.

"An old girlfriend?" Jake inquired as he stacked Sean's empty plates, one on the other.

"You could kind of say that, too," Sean affirmed.

"Sounds like it's kinda troublesome," Jake persisted. "But girls can be like that. Sometimes they're not the most rational."

Sean nodded. "No," he pronounced, adapting his most serious tone of voice. "Girls are not rational. At all."

Zoey and Nina stood in silence as they watched Aisha's ferry pull out of the dock.

"I feel like it's the forties, and we're watching our old buddy go off to war," Nina mused. She'd been struggling for something innocuous to say, something non-Lucas related.

"Yeah," Zoey said solemnly.

"Want some cereal?" Nina asked, holding the half-eaten box out to Zoey.

"No way!" Zoey laughed. "If I eat those before I go jogging, there will be rainbow barf to account for!"

Nina laughed, too. "Well, I guess I'm going to head home," she said. "Maybe go back to bed."

Zoey shot her a pitying glance. "Oh, Nina!" she cried. "I know you're really upset about Benjamin, but that's no reason to hang around in a dark room all day."

Nina was mute. Benjamin? She'd barely thought about Benjamin. "Look," Zoey comforted, swinging her arm around Nina's shoulders. "I won't go jogging if you won't just go home and sulk. We can hang out at my house for a while, maybe go to the beach. Or you could come with me to see Lucas. I'm meeting him for lunch. I could make a picnic for the three of us. What do you say?"

At the thought of seeing Lucas, Nina felt a surge of warmth through her body. It felt like ages since she'd last seen him, although it was only last night at the mall.

She glanced over at Zoey's expectant face, and the warmth she'd felt turned cold. "I—I—I can't," she stammered. "I've got to have lunch with my dad. He's coming home from work to talk to me."

She was lying, of course. She was lying to her best friend.

107

Twelve

Not even the sound of falling rain could help Claire fall asleep.

An avid student of weather, there was nothing Claire found more soothing than precipitation. That's why she'd ordered the boxed set of CDs from the American Weather Institute. Each CD featured the sounds of a different rainstorm. Claire's favorite was *Tropical Rainstorm in Congo Brush Field.*

Sometimes Claire would lie back in bed with the CD on automatic repeat and imagine herself standing amidst the long blades of hot grass, her long black hair streaming down her back, her summer dress sticking to her. Claire would fantasize that she was in the Amazon, doing research as a world-renowned climatologist, or sometimes—during more romantically inclined moments—she'd imagine Aaron showing up, a single white rose in his hand.

After Claire had received last night's note, she'd put on the CDs. Yet still she'd lain awake.

At some point in the night Claire made a resolution. She needed to tell someone.

It had gone too far. She couldn't do this alone.

Claire looked up at the itinerary she had posted to her bulletin board, and her eyes combed the long list of cities and venues. Today Aaron's band was in Atlanta.

"Peachtree Hotel," the switchboard operator answered.

"Hello," Claire said. She was amazed to hear how awake she could make herself sound. "May I please be connected with Aaron Mendel?"

Claire heard the woman tapping on a keyboard. "That's *M-e-n-d-e-l?*" she asked.

"Yes," Claire replied.

"I'm sorry, ma'am, but there's nobody here registered under that name." Claire was momentarily stricken—where was Aaron? Then she remembered.

"What about *K-i-n-c-a-i-d?*" she asked, recalling a recent conversation with Aaron. "I'm gonna start registering under a fake name. To protect myself from fans," he'd said. Claire had laughed. The band was barely out of high school. They barely had fans!

"I'll connect you," the receptionist relayed.

Claire listened to a couple of ads for the hotel's rooftop restaurants and the beginning strains to a popular light FM song before she was finally connected to the band's room.

"Hello!" someone screamed. "If this is room service, you're late!" Claire could hear the thrashing sounds of guitars being tuned in the background.

"It's not room service!" Claire strained her tired vocal cords in an attempt to speak above the ruckus on the other end of the receiver. "It's Claire!" she yelled. "Is Aaron there?"

Claire listened as whoever it was who answered the phone—probably some surly roadie they'd met on the way—dropped the receiver unceremoniously and shouted: "Mendel, man, it's some chick for you!"

Claire grimaced. Sometimes guys in bands were the worst.

"I hope you didn't hear that." It was Aaron.

"Well, I did," Claire prickled. "But it's okay."

"Dumb guy stuff," Aaron apologized. "You know . . ."

"Forget it. I have more important things to talk about," Claire stated. She needed to get to the point. And fast.

"Sure, babe," Aaron replied. "But I've got a photo crew about to come over to take my picture for *Atlanta Underground.* It's a local music magazine here."

Claire didn't want to hear about it. "Aaron!" she implored. "I've got to tell you something! *Now!*"

There was silence on the other end of the line. "Okay," he said.

Claire took a deep breath. Now that she had his attention, she almost didn't want to tell him. It was so hard to get it out. "Well, here goes," she began. There was a loud crashing noise in the background.

Claire waited.

"Someone just spilled a Coke on one of the drums," Aaron explained. "Just ignore it. Tell me what's going on."

"Okay, w-well," Claire stammered. She took a deep breath. "I'm being stalked." The minute that she said it, she wanted to take it back. It sounded ridiculous.

"You're being what?" Aaron asked. "You're being walked?" There was more noise in the background. Claire could hear the doorbell ringing and some guy practically screaming, "Room service dude! It's about time!"

"Not *walked*," Claire corrected. "Stalked! I'm being *stalked.*" This time she said each word slowly and deliberately.

There was a pause.

"What do you mean?" Aaron sounded beyond incredulous.

Claire took Aaron through the list of recent events, ending with the previous night's shopping bag sabotage. When she'd finally finished, she waited for his response. She could feel her grip tightening on the phone. *He's going to want to come home right away. I'll have to tell him that it's not a big deal, that I can handle it. But he'll insist.* That was fine. All she really wanted was his comforting words. Claire waited.

And waited.

Finally Aaron spoke. "Claire," he began. "Are you sure this isn't just some elaborate practical joke? I mean, come on, who would stalk you?"

"I don't call shredding each and every item of clothing in my closet funny!" Claire cried. She'd meant to scream, but she was so tired, it had come out more like a yelp. "I don't call receiving a dead mouse in an old shoe box hilarious, do you, Aaron?"

Claire was overwhelmed once again by the sounds of chaos on the other end of the line. She heard a doorbell, then a cackle of new voices—some of them female—and the sound of furniture moving. "Claire, it's the photographer and her crew!" Aaron called. "They're here!"

Claire was silent. She didn't know what to say.

"Can I call you later?" Aaron asked. "We'll talk about this then. But really, babe, I don't think you have to worry."

"Okay," Claire said sharply.

"I love you," were Aaron's final words before he hung up.

Claire lay curled up in a little ball on the bed, the covers pulled all the way to her neck. The cordless phone was still in her quivering hands.

111

She was feeling a million different things at once. Fear. Anger. Disappointment. But more than anything else, she was feeling determination. Calling Aaron had obviously been a mistake. He'd been too consumed in his own surroundings to pay attention, yet somehow his disbelief, his nonchalance, had mobilized her.

She had to tell somebody what was going on. She needed a partner to do away with this mouse-leaving, clothes-shredding stalker from hell.

Claire pressed talk and listened for the dial tone. Then she dialed the first numbers that came to her.

Benjamin was looking for a reason to leave the house, so when Claire called and told him it was a matter of dire consequence that she see him, he was relieved to change out of the pajamas he'd been wearing all morning and put on a clean T-shirt and jeans.

Benjamin had tried to get to Claire's as quickly as possible, but making his way down Camden Road posed quite a challenge. His legs felt wobbly, and he still suffered from shooting pains up and down his back and shoulders. Maybe if he just took it easy for a week or so, everything would get better. Then he'd be back to his old surfing self. . . .

Benjamin stood before the Geiger house. It had been a while since he'd been there. *What if Nina's in the kitchen and I have to pass her on my way upstairs?* Benjamin wondered. He put his foot on the bottom step and paused for a second. He felt suddenly wistful and was overcome with the desire to see Nina. Maybe she'd be reading one of her fanzines on the living-room couch or eating a bowl of soggy cereal at the kitchen table or watching television in her room. He bounded up the front steps. *It will be fun to hang out with Nina,* he thought eagerly. Then he remembered.

He wasn't there for Nina. He was there for Claire.

Benjamin knocked on the door. No one came. He knocked harder, pelting the wood frame door with his clenched fist. Nothing. Not only was Nina not around, but Claire wasn't, either! *How Claire,* he thought. *She tells me she needs to see me urgently, then she takes off without leaving a note.*

Benjamin was dreading the walk back home, and his knees buckled at the thought of the return trip. But just as he was turning to go, he heard a whisper from inside the house.

"Benjamin, is that you?" Claire hissed.

"Of course it's me!" Benjamin clamored. "You asked me to come over, remember?"

Benjamin listened as Claire unlocked the two double locks, then undid the chain. What the hell was going on? No one on the island ever kept their doors locked.

"Sorry," Claire said, looking over Benjamin's shoulder.

Benjamin tried to hide in his face the fact that he was a bit shocked by Claire's appearance. She was usually in perfect form—hair combed back, skin freshly scrubbed, clothes ironed. Now her hair was a tangled mess. And the circles under her eyes—they were so pronounced, it looked as if she had two black eyes. The only thing that saved her from looking like a complete disaster was the clothes she had on. They were brightly colored and crisply ironed. They looked brand-new.

"Benjamin, I can't tell you how much I appreciate your coming here. I really needed someone," Claire murmured in an uncharacteristic display of gratitude. Claire really wasn't being herself.

"Claire, don't worry about it, but I gotta know . . .

what's going on?" Benjamin asked. They were walking up the stairs to Claire's room.

"I'll tell you in a second," she whispered conspiratorially. It was as if she thought someone was there who might hear them, but as far as Benjamin could tell, not even Janelle, the maid, was in the house.

Claire led Benjamin to the widow's walk above her room. Climbing the ladder, Benjamin miscalculated the space between rungs and nearly fell.

"Are you okay?" Claire asked, grabbing at his T-shirt.

"Yeah, yeah," Benjamin answered. "Just lost my balance or something. No big deal."

Benjamin felt relieved once they were outside, but he was eager to know why he'd been summoned. "Okay, Claire, explain now," he begged. "This is making me nuts!"

Claire emitted a long and heavy sigh. "Well," she began. "Here goes. . . ."

It took a long time for Claire to tell her tale and for Benjamin to get in all his questions. By the time she was through, the sun was beginning to dim across the island.

"Benjamin," Claire said quietly. "I know I haven't always been the greatest friend. But I need you now. I have a few ideas, but I can't get rid of this guy alone."

Benjamin had been so absorbed in Claire's story, he'd forgotten how much his body ached. This was the first time that had happened since the accident.

"I'll help you, Claire," he promised. "We'll get this guy. We'll find out who he is, and we'll stop him."

Nina

What's up with the Spice
Girls? Is it just me or what?
I mean, I'm not sure if
they're a rock group or a bunch
of Smurf rejects. Remember how
the Smurfs had names that
were defined by their personali-
ties? Dopey Smurf, Sleepy
Smurf, Brainy Smurf, and ... I
don't remember any others. Well,
the Spice Girls are barely a hop,
skip, and jump away from
Smurfdom, as far as I'm concerned. I mean, there's Hot
Spice, Wild Spice, Sporty Spice.
I'm waiting for Old Spice —the
swarthy seafaring Spice Girl

with an eye patch. I guess the idea is to pick the biggest guiding thing in your life, and then define yourself by it.

It's a fun game. Anybody can be a Spice Girl. Watch:

Zoey Passmore: Sugar 'n' Spice
Aisha Gray: Intellectual Spice
Jake McRoyan: Burly Spice
Claire Geiger: Cold as Spice

Isn't that great? We could have a TV show, detailing all our wacky Spicecapades! And I could be the star.

But who'd want to watch a show about Crappy Friend Spice?

JAKE

What's up with this uni-sex perfume craze? Okay, maybe I'm too macho or something, but I don't get it. I'm not going to wear the same perfume as Kate. Does that make me insensitive? I'm not sure. And what's up with those commercials? A bunch of stringy, unappealing girls and weird-looking guys standing in a row. They all look kind of dirty to me. I mean, those people barely look like they can get it together to take a shower, much less buy a sixty-dollar bottle of perfume. That crowd doesn't seem to have a major stake in personal hygiene, but whatever.

Advertising has gotten weird. Everybody in "high fashion" looks incredibly listless all of a sudden. I don't know; personally, I like people to look happy and healthy.

Is there something wrong with that?

Thirteen

"Please don't sit next to me. Please don't sit next to me," Aisha muttered under her breath as the line of passengers filed onto the bus bound for Boston.

Aisha did her best to make herself as unappealing looking a travel companion as possible. She slurped loudly from the cappuccino she'd gotten at the stand outside the station, intermittently digging her hand into a bag of caramel-coated popcorn she'd purchased.

She placed a pile of books, notebooks, and maps on the seat next to her. *Someone would have to be really pushy to ask me to move all this stuff,* Aisha thought.

It wasn't that Aisha hated people. It was just that she had too much to do to spend the three-hour trip from North Harbor to Boston making small talk. And wasn't it always some saccharine-sweet old granny who sat next to you and offered you butterscotch sucking candy from her purse and told you endless anecdotes about her eleven grandchildren?

Aisha had no intention of wasting her trip. She had lists to make, plans to concoct. As she took the last sip of the lukewarm milky coffee she picked up her composition notebook and opened it to the first empty page. She began writing.

What to Ask Carina Connelly When You Meet Her

1. Tell me about your relationship with Christopher Shupe.
2. Were you in love with him?
3. Why did you get married so early?
4. Would you still like to be married?
5. Are you still in love with him?
6. Are you really a drug addict?

Aisha mulled over the list. Maybe the last question was a little much. She was contemplating crossing it out when she had the distinct feeling that someone was watching her. Aisha looked up. There was a guy standing over her.

"Is someone sitting here?" he asked. Aisha could hear that he had a flagrant Boston accent. He'd sounded like he'd said: "Is somebody sitting heeyah?"

Aisha thought about composing a lie, but he'd caught her off guard. Anyway, he was cute—in a kind of nerdy way. He had bright red hair, and he wore little tortoiseshell horn-rimmed glasses, a maroon sweatshirt with Harvard Rugby written over the left breast, and jeans. He looked about Aisha's age, maybe a couple of years older.

"I said: Is somebody sitting here?" he repeated.

"N-No," Aisha muttered. She moved her pile of books out of the seat.

Well, at least he wasn't an old lady.

Lucas hadn't planned on getting off the boat for lunch, even though that's what all the other guys did after a morning at sea. But when he pulled into the docks and saw Zoey—her cheeks flushed from the sea air, a wicker picnic basket in her hand—he saw that he'd have to.

"Ain't that your little lassie?" one of the older fishermen asked him with a grin.

Lucas was a little shocked to see Zoey standing there. There was something almost vulnerable about the way she looked, standing on the docks by herself, and Lucas felt a flash of guilt. Here was this girl, his girlfriend, surprising him with a picnic lunch.

He didn't deserve her.

"So what are you going to be doing in Boston?" Aisha's bus companion asked.

"Research," Aisha answered. She knew it was an oblique response, but somehow she didn't think she could tell a complete stranger the real story behind her voyage—even if he did look like a pretty up-and-up guy. He'd introduced himself as Graham, a second-year graduate student at Harvard, studying chemistry, who was from Somerville, Mass., just near Cambridge. He'd been visiting a friend in Augusta.

Graham didn't seem particularly fazed by her answer. "So if you don't mind my asking, how come you chose Princeton over Harvard?" Graham inquired, shifting so that he could rest his right elbow on the back of the seat in front of him and look Aisha directly in the eye.

"I wasn't accepted at Harvard," Aisha answered. "I don't really know why."

"Hmm. Too bad," Graham said with a little smile.

"We could use some more girls walking around the science quads. It can get pretty dreary."

Aisha smiled. Nothing better to get her mind off her troubles than a little harmless flirting.

Lucas watched as Zoey popped a green grape in her mouth.

"Zo, you really didn't have to do this," he murmured. He put the sandwich he was eating down on the ground next to him so his hands were free to caress the side of Zoey's cheek. Her skin felt soft and hot. He noticed that the minute he touched her, her neck went limp and her eyelids began to flutter.

Lucas gave Zoey a quick kiss on the lips. "What was that for?" she asked.

"What? I'm not allowed to kiss my girlfriend?" Lucas asked, pretending to be affronted.

"Well," Zoey replied, "it's just that you've seemed sort of distracted lately. . . ."

Lucas was getting ready to apologize when he heard a whistling sound coming from the boat. It was one of the older fishermen. "Hey, Cabral, no more puppy love! It's time to get back to work!" the guy screamed.

"Daddy wouldn't like you kissin' on the job!" another fisherman called.

"Those guys watch me every second of the day." Lucas bristled. "Man, I can't stand it!" he exclaimed.

"Don't worry about it," Zoey comforted, nuzzling him. "They're just a bunch of old uneducated goons. What do they know?"

As fast as Zoey had eaten that grape, Lucas felt all the warmth he'd felt moments ago subside. *Doesn't she realize,* he thought mournfully, *that one day I'm going to be one of those old uneducated goons?*

Aisha had been on the bus for two and a half hours,

but she hadn't done any more work on what she secretly named "the Connelly Caper." She'd talked to Graham nonstop for the entire bus trip.

"I can't believe you didn't get into Harvard," he kept saying. "I mean, from what you say, you sound incredibly qualified. And they have a terrific astronomy program. I know they're looking for female applicants. I mean, there aren't that many women scientists." He paused. "And certainly none as pretty as you," he added.

Aisha blushed. This guy was now officially flirting with her. "Well, maybe I'll transfer after a year," she offered. "If Princeton doesn't work out."

"Or better yet," Graham countered, "you could apply now to get in second semester! Why even bother with Princeton?"

Aisha giggled. God, Harvard people could be so snobby. But this guy did have a right to be confident. He seemed really smart, and he was cute. The nerd thing was really beginning to rub off on her. *And,* she thought, *he probably doesn't have any skeletons in the closet . . . he probably doesn't have a wife somewhere. I probably know more about this guy after one bus ride than I've ever known about Christopher!*

Aisha had a momentary fantasy: Maybe she'd forget about chasing after Carina. Who cared, anyway? Couldn't she just try to forget about Christopher? Chalk the whole thing up to a horrible learning experience? She could use this trip to Boston as a way to get to know Graham. . . .

"Zo, I gotta go back to work," Lucas grumbled. He tried not to be too abrupt, he tried not to spoil the mood, but he couldn't help it. He was pissed.

"Lucas, don't let those guys spoil our time!" Zoey cried. "They're just miserable old men whose entire lives revolve around their pathetic fishing boats!"

The minute Zoey said that, she slapped her hand over her mouth. Lucas looked at the shattered expression on the face he'd been caressing moments ago. He knew she felt bad, but he just couldn't get it out of his head. "Pathetic fishing boats" was a phrase that wouldn't leave his mind easily. Zoey just didn't understand. *Those guys are my future,* Lucas thought drearily. *That miserable life is soon to be mine.*

"Zo, if you think those guys are miserable, what do you think my life is going to be like?" Lucas asked. He stood up and brushed the dirt from the dock off his jeans.

"Lucas, I didn't mean that how it sounded! You know I didn't!" Zoey protested.

"Uh-huh," Lucas replied. He knew Zoey hadn't directed her comments at him, but they made him feel wretched, anyway.

"Lucas, I swear," Zoey cried. "I love you! I think what you're doing is great! I think it's amazing!"

"I gotta go," Lucas grumbled. Part of him hated leaving her standing there upset and alone, but another part of him felt like he had to get out of there fast, before everything got worse.

I'm doing it again! Lucas thought, remembering how sweet Zoey had looked when he'd gotten off the boat. That had been only a half an hour ago. *I'm making this big deal out of nothing. I'm making her feel like everything that's wrong between us is her fault when really it's mine. God, why did I have to screw up so badly?*

"Lucas!" Zoey exclaimed. "I feel like you just got mad at me over absolutely nothing!" He didn't say anything. "Please tell me," she implored. "Is there something else you're upset about?"

It was as if she were reading his mind.

Aisha was telling an anecdote regarding her astronomy lab teacher, and she was gesticulating wildly. It was a habit she had: When her stories got animated, her hands went all over the place.

"Uh, can I ask you something?" Graham asked all of a sudden. Aisha heard a tentativeness in his voice that she hadn't heard before.

"Sure," Aisha answered. "Ask away!"

"That ring," Graham commented, pointing to Aisha's left hand. "Is that a wedding ring?"

Aisha was at a loss. She wanted to lie, but she couldn't.

"I guess your silence means yes," Graham said when Aisha failed to respond.

"En-Engagement," Aisha stammered. She'd meant to take the thing off last night. Why had she left it on?

"Wow." Graham's eyes grew large. "I just never think of people your age being hitched. Or almost hitched."

Aisha shrugged awkwardly.

"Sorry," Graham apologized. "Is *hitched* a word with negative connotations or something? I feel like I just insulted you."

"No, you didn't insult me." Aisha clutched her notebooks to her tightly.

"Oh, okay." Graham smiled. "Because insulting you is the last thing I'd want to do."

"Oh, yeah?" Aisha asked coyly.

"Yeah," Graham responded. "Well, second to last. I wouldn't want to accidentally drop something heavy on you, either."

Aisha offered up a weak smile. She and Graham began talking about their favorite science publications. For the rest of the trip they struggled to regain the momentum that their conversation had held during the first couple of hours of the trip.

But it was impossible to get it back. Eventually they stopped trying to talk and rode the last leg of the voyage in silence.

Claire

What's up with all these movies about natural disasters? I hate to say it, but they give weather a bad name. Like *Twister*. I know that most people thought the storm chasers in that movie were crazy, but I really identified with them. I love the sheer power of a natural catastrophe—the unrelenting force of it.

Like that old commercial says, "It's not nice to fool with Mother Nature."

I like to think Ms. Nature and I have something in common.

LUCAS

What's up with guys who have affairs? Like on those soap operas my mom watches during the day. There are always these guys with greased-back hair and names like Duke who are married to one woman and going out with another woman. They wake up with their wives and then sneak off to be with their mistresses. If you ask me, that's a whole lot more trouble than it's worth. I can barely handle the fact that I kissed someone else while I was going out with Zoey. I mean, I just never want it to happen again. Not that I'm even sure how it happened. Or why. Or what I'm supposed to do about it.

I'm just not sure about anything anymore.

Fourteen

Christopher knocked on the door to the Gray Inn. He hoped Aisha would answer it. He loved her family and all, but he'd come to see her. He wasn't in the mood for chat about the weather with Mr. Gray, and he definitely wasn't up for a game of Sega football with Kalif.

He needed to talk to Aisha. It was time they had everything out.

"Hi, Christopher." Mrs. Gray smiled at him. Christopher gave her a kiss on the cheek. "Don't get too close!" she warned. "I have flour all over me. Your little sister and I are making cookies for the guests."

Christopher nodded. "I take it you're here to see your sister," Mrs. Gray added, wiping her hands on her apron and ushering Christopher into the house.

"Uh, no," Christopher replied. That was odd. Aisha's mother knew he lived with Kendra. Why would he want to come and see her?

But Mrs. Gray looked confused. "Then what brings you here?" she asked.

"Well, uh," Christopher stuttered. "I was kinda hoping to see Eesh."

"Eesh?" Mrs. Gray repeated. "Christopher, don't be silly."

"What do you mean?" Christopher asked. He loved

his girlfriend's mother, but had she completely lost it?

"Did you forget that Aisha's gone away?" Mrs. Gray replied.

Christopher heard Mrs. Gray's words, but it took him a minute to register them.

It was a good thing Zoey still had her jogging clothes on because after her bout with Lucas, she'd needed to talk to somebody urgently. Having just spilled her guts to Nina the day before, she would have preferred to talk to Aisha, but unfortunately she wasn't around. She felt a bit guilty about burdening Nina with all her problems, mostly when it was so obvious that Nina herself was pretty devastated over Benjamin. But what could she do?

Zoey needed a friend. Desperately.

Zoey had a sense of déjà vu as she knocked on Nina's door repeatedly. She could hear the television booming.

"Nina, are you there?" she called out.

"Zo, don't you know you're interrupting my sacred viewing time?" Nina gave a mock groan as she came to the door. "Hello, don't you know that *Samurai Pizza Kids* is on?"

Zoey smiled weakly at her friend and all her quirks. She wanted to laugh, but right now she needed Nina's other qualities—her compassion, her ability to read situations and analyze people.

"Nina," she said patiently. "This is important."

"Yes, Christopher," Mrs. Gray informed him. "Aisha's at Princeton looking at housing."

"Uh, right." Christopher tried desperately to sound convincing. "I must have forgotten."

"Poor thing!" Mrs. Gray cried. "You really must be working too hard. You know, I asked Eesh, I said,

129

'Honey, why don't you have Christopher go with you?' I thought you could accompany her, Christopher, on the condition that you bunked in the men's dorms, of course." She winked. "But Aisha said you were too busy at work," Mrs. Gray added.

"Oh, yeah, I am," Christopher commented. "Really busy."

Christopher followed Mrs. Gray into the kitchen, where he was deliciously overwhelmed by the smell of chocolate chip cookies baking. "I asked Aisha to call the minute she got to Princeton," Mrs. Gray was saying. "Between you and me, Christopher," she whispered, "I wish Eesh were going to school a little bit closer to home. But at least New Jersey's not as far away as California. Poor Darla and Jeff Passmore." Mrs. Gray sighed.

Christopher tried his hardest to pay close attention to Mrs. Gray's words, but his mind was racing. Aisha had never mentioned anything about going to Princeton to him.

Christopher had the sinking feeling she'd gone somewhere else.

"Maybe you should just give him some time alone, Zo," Nina recommended. She was sprawled on her bed, absently staring at the muted television set. Zoey knew that she'd just barged in, but she wished Nina would turn off the TV altogether. She felt her problems with Lucas deserved her best friend's complete attention.

"Nina, you act like I'm smothering him," Zoey said. She was sitting on the floor, digging her fingers into the carpeting.

"I didn't say that, Zo," Nina countered. "It's just that the guy did just go through some major stuff. I mean, his dad died, and he's bummed about staying around here—"

Zoey cut her off. "Nina, I feel like I keep hurting his feelings by accident, and he won't let me apologize. Am I that insensitive? Every time I see him, I say the wrong thing! I could try to give him some space, but then I keep thinking that time's running out. I mean, I'm leaving for California soon. If Lucas and I don't spend time together now, when are we going to spend time together?"

Nina was silent. "I don't know, Zo."

Usually Nina has an opinion on everything, Zoey thought. *Why is it that suddenly she's mute? Could it be that she's too wrapped up in her own problems to give me any real advice?* Zoey wondered. *Maybe it's too hard for her to talk about this because she can't deal with what happened between her and Benjamin.*

"I guess I wish you were more surprised," Zoey said finally. She was trying to stifle any feelings of anger toward Nina, but she had to admit to herself that she was feeling a few. Couldn't Nina see beyond herself and her own problems for a second? "I mean, don't you think it's horrible that Lucas doesn't want to see me?"

Zoey observed Nina's expressions as she composed her answer. Her best friend looked exasperated as her gray eyes darted around nervously, and her lips curled downward. She was no longer gazing at the television set but was sitting up in her bed, absentmindedly twirling a loose thread from her quilt around her right index finger.

"I'm just trying to say that Lucas probably has a lot on his mind," Nina finally said. "That's all."

Zoey watched Nina continue to curl the thread around her finger. She was pulling it tighter and tighter, and her stubby little finger looked red and swollen. She looked like she was hurting herself.

Zoey wondered briefly whether Nina could even feel the pain.

Christopher was sampling one of Mrs. Gray's cookies. "Not too chewy, right?" she was asking. He nodded, his mouth full. "And what about the chocolate chips? Did I make the right move using dark instead of milk?"

Christopher nodded again. The sweetness of the cookies was doing nothing to counter the sour taste in his mouth. Where was Aisha?

"Well, if it isn't Miss Kendra," Mrs. Gray said suddenly. Christopher turned to see his little sister walking into the room. She was carrying a bag of groceries from the corner market. Christopher couldn't help noticing that she averted her eyes when she saw him.

"They didn't have two percent milk, Mrs. Gray. Only skim," she was saying.

"Oh, dear," Mrs. Gray responded. "The guests always complain when there's only skim for the coffee," she said, and then shrugged. "Oh, well. I have some more straightening to do." She removed her apron and paused. "If you're not here when I get back, it was nice to see you, Christopher," she said warmly. "I'm sure we'll see a lot more of you when Aisha's back in town."

"Thanks for the cookies, Mrs. Gray," Christopher replied. He watched as Aisha's mother left the kitchen. He waited until she was out of earshot and turned to Kendra.

"All right, sis," he growled. "Now spill!"

Zoey couldn't believe it. She'd gone to Nina for comfort, and now she felt even worse. She was starting to feel a little paranoid.

"Look, Nina," she exclaimed. "I just don't get it! Why are you on Lucas's side?"

"Zoey!" Nina cried defensively. "I'm not on Lucas's side! I'm on your side."

"Not that there are sides," Zoey corrected herself. "I just feel like you're sympathizing more with Lucas." She paused. "Which, I guess, would make sense. I mean, he's going through such a hard time."

"Am I saying the wrong thing? Am I being a bad friend?" Nina's eyes were so watery, they looked almost charcoal colored. Zoey could tell she'd upset her.

"It's okay, Nina." Zoey reached for Nina's hands. "I'm not doing such a great job right now, either."

"I'm sorry," Nina apologized. "Please don't be mad. I don't know what's wrong with me—"

"And I'm sorry, too," Zoey said. She paused for a minute, then asked, "Why does everything keep getting all mixed up? Am I missing something?"

Nina didn't say anything.

Christopher didn't have time to play games. He opened fire with a direct threat.

"Kendra," he said slowly. "Tell me where Aisha is. Right now." He was standing over his little sister, and he could feel her quivering. He'd nearly exploded at her the other day, when he'd found out that she'd told Aisha about Carina. He knew she'd do anything not to have that happen again.

"I—I—I don't know where Aisha is," she stuttered. "Please, don't ask me." Christopher could tell by the quaking in Kendra's voice that she was lying.

"I know she's not at Princeton," Christopher said. "I know she's not looking at housing." Kendra didn't say anything. "And I know that you know where she really is."

Kendra bowed her head so that all Christopher could see was the perfect part in the middle of her scalp. Her curls were hanging down around her face. "Don't avoid my eyes," Christopher warned her. "You always avoid making eye contact when you're lying. You've been doing it since you were a little kid!"

"Christopher, I'm telling you the truth," Kendra said, looking up suddenly. "I don't know where Aisha is. At least . . . I don't know exactly."

Nina finally made a suggestion.

"Zoey," she said. "Look, I know I keep messing up here, but I just think Lucas is a really intense person. From what you're telling me, it seems like he's pretty messed up about everything. Maybe you should just concentrate on showing Lucas a good time. You know, making sure he's having fun."

"Well, we went to the movies, and that was good," Zoey affirmed. "And the picnic would have been fine if those old guys hadn't gotten on Lucas's nerves. . . ." Zoey contemplated the recent events. "I know," she said suddenly. "What about a party? At my house. Something really casual—like a barbecue or some-thing. You could help me set it up—you and Lucas. That way we could all spend some time together. And it wouldn't be so serious. There's no way that Lucas and I could get into a fight."

"Oh, Zoey, another party? But you just had one," Nina complained. "I was thinking that maybe you and Lucas should go to an amusement park together or something. Not drag us all into it."

"Well," Zoey said, "I'll be killing two birds with one stone, won't I?"

"What do you mean?" Nina asked.

"Lucas will have a good time," Zoey offered. "And you'll get out of the house. No offense, Nina, but it's obvious you need to!"

Zoey was thrilled with her plan.

Fifteen

8:30 a.m.

Aisha woke up in a strange bed in a strange room. She'd left the TV on all night, and the sheets smelled musty. It took her a few minutes to remember: She'd spent the night at the Hello, Boston! motel.

9:30 a.m.

Jake served another egg white omelette with dry wheat toast to the same strange guy who'd come in the day before. The guy left him a medium-size tip.

10:00 a.m.

Claire sat in front of the computer screen. Her fingers hit the keyboard with hard purposeful strokes as she composed a plan of action for herself and Benjamin. For the first time in a long time, Claire was smiling.

10:30 a.m.

Zoey perused the aisles of the grocery store. She couldn't decide which barbecue sauce to get, so she bought them both.

11:00 a.m.

Kate was sick of developing pictures. She wanted to go visit Jake at Burger Heaven, but she knew it probably wasn't a very good idea. Max would be there, giving her the evil eye. But she really wanted a cup of coffee. She'd just get one to go.

12:00 p.m.

Nina woke up.

12:20 p.m.

The little wooden chair wobbled as Sean sat down. He turned on his laptop computer and waited for it to boot up. He loved the way the screen cast a warm glow across the motel room. It reminded him of home.

12:30 p.m.

Nina couldn't find the remote control.

1:00 p.m.

Benjamin sat in the lobby of the eye doctor, full of dread. He didn't want to tell the guy he hadn't followed his advice. He'd overdone it. He'd taken the surfing thing too far. And now his body ached and his head hurt. He hoped the migraines were unrelated.

1:01 p.m.

Nina found the remote control.

2:00 p.m.

Aisha called her mom from a pay phone on Beacon Street. "Hey, Mom," she said. "Yeah, it's nice here. No, I'm not sure which dorm is right for me. No, I don't know who my roommate is going to be." She paused. "Christopher came over? He did? Of course I told him where I was going. He just forgot." There was a rush of sirens in the background. "Mom, don't worry! There's just the . . . uh . . . Squirrel Patrol Squad. No—no, they're not rabid! They're just—noisy. Look, I gotta go!" She hung up the phone. That had worked. She hoped.

2:30 p.m.

Claire was still typing away busily. Suddenly she stopped and stared at the words she'd written. She tried to type some more, but the screen was frozen. Again. "Oh, God," she gasped. "How could I have been so stupid? Now I need to come up with another plan."

2:31 p.m.

Sean's computer made a harsh beeping sound as he logged off the network. Sean chuckled as he disconnected the modem from the back of his computer. He needed to recharge the cell phone battery he used to log into the network. He'd need it for later.

3:00 p.m.

Zoey pored over the cookbook. Spareribs or chicken breasts? That was the question.

3:30 p.m.

Lucas left work early, thanks to the wind, which was exceptionally fierce. He walked along the docks aimlessly for a while. He couldn't figure out why he'd been so harsh to Zoey yesterday. He wanted to talk to someone about it. The only problem was that the person he most wanted to talk to was Nina.

3:45 p.m.

Lara saw Lucas walking aimlessly down Center Street. She followed him.

4:00 p.m.

Nina was happy. *Samurai Pizza Kids* was on. She'd missed most of it yesterday. "I wonder if Lucas would think this is as amusing as I do," she wondered.

5:00 p.m.

"Zoey called," Mrs. Cabral said as Lucas walked in the front door. "She said you need to be at a barbecue at her house this evening. And she won't take no for an answer!" The fact that Zoey was giving him another chance after he'd been so mean yesterday—it made him feel even worse.

5:01 p.m.

Lara stood outside Lucas's house. She was waiting, although she wasn't sure what for.

5:30 p.m.

Jake tried not to show his irritation with Kate. She had sat at Burger Heaven for his entire shift. Although she'd been pretending to read the paper, he'd felt her eyes on him the whole time. At least she wasn't crying.

6:58 p.m.

Claire decided to go out for a walk. She felt like exercising her rediscovered freedom. She walked down Center Street toward town. She felt fine until she hit the corner of Center and Sheffield, where she was momentarily blinded by a white flash of light.

7:00 p.m.

Sean crouched in his hiding place on the corner of Sheffield and Center. He held his Polaroid camera in one hand and the just developed picture in the other. He'd forgotten about the flash.

7:30 p.m.

Lara finally went home. But she wasn't giving up.

Sixteen

Aisha stood before the dilapidated four-level apartment complex. It didn't look so different from the Hello, Boston! motel, where she'd spent the previous night. The outer walls were composed of dirty white shingles, and each unit had its own entrance with a tattered blue awning and a dirty welcome mat.

Aisha knew that Carina Connelly resided in apartment three, which was on the second level. Aisha had even gone so far as to stand outside the door, listening if anyone was home. She was pretty certain somebody was because she could hear the television blaring—the *Sesame Street* theme song. Why was Carina Connelly watching children's television?

The one thing Aisha hadn't done yet was knock on Carina's door. She'd prepared herself for the dreaded move more than a few times—she'd combed down her hair, checked her reflection in her compact mirror, practiced her opening lines in her head over and over again: "Hello, my name is Aisha Gray. May I come in and ask you a few questions?" But she wasn't exactly sure she *wanted* to know the answers.

Aisha had tried to psych herself up. *The sooner you knock, the sooner you know,* she told herself. But something held her back.

"Gutless Wonder," she muttered to herself as she walked down Carina's street. She figured that maybe if she just walked around the block a couple of times, she'd get over herself. *You didn't come all this way for a stroll,* Aisha grumbled silently.

Aisha decided to stop inside the deli around the corner. Maybe a little refreshment was all she needed. She went inside, ordered a cup of coffee, and sat at the picnic table set up on the outside lawn. She read the Lifestyles section of *The Boston Globe* to pass the time.

"Can I get you a refill?" the proprietor asked. Aisha had barely finished her first cup, but she wasn't about to turn down an offer for an energy recharge.

"Sure," she answered. "Bring on the caffeine."

"You a student?" the guy asked. Aisha had noticed him working behind the deli counter when she'd gone in to buy her coffee. He was an old bald man wearing a white apron. It was smeared with mustard and ketchup and a variety of other condiments. Aisha tried not to get grossed out.

"I'm a student," Aisha answered. "Yes."

"Harvard?" the deli man asked. "Or shall I correct myself: Hahvahd?" He grinned as he made fun of the Boston accent. Aisha had a momentary pang as she thought of Graham.

"No, not Harvard." She laughed. "I'm going to Princeton in the fall."

"Princeton!" The man's eyebrows shot up. "Then I hate to tell you—you're lost!"

Aisha laughed politely. She took a sip of coffee before she responded. "I'm trying to find a friend in the area," she commented. "Actually," she corrected herself, "it's a friend of my fiancé's. You see, we're getting married soon, and I know he'd love it if she

141

were at the wedding. The thing is, we've been unable to locate her. So I came to track her down. I know she lives around here, and I'm just waiting for her to get home."

"I hope you don't mind my asking . . . ," the guy said.

But you're going to ask, anyway, Aisha thought, *even if I do mind.*

"But what's this woman's name?"

"Why?" Aisha stumbled. "You don't think you know her, do you?"

"Boston's a lot smaller than you think." The deli man laughed. "Sometimes it seems to me that there are round about twenty people in the entire city."

Go for it, Aisha told herself. *Just tell him. How could it hurt?* "Her name is Carina Connelly," Aisha answered. It surprised her how nonchalantly she was able to say the sentence. The name Carina Connelly seemed to roll off her lips.

Aisha looked at the deli man. What was that expression on his face? Concentration? Concern? "Do you know her?" she asked.

"Yes," he answered. His tone was formal all of a sudden. "I know her."

Aisha could barely contain herself. Never in her wildest dreams had she thought someone would actually know Carina. Here was her chance to get the real dirt—before she met Carina face-to-face. "That's—great. Could you tell me about her?" Aisha begged.

"You sure you're a student?" the man asked, suddenly suspicious.

Who does he think I am, Aisha thought incredulously, *the feds?*

"I'm sure," Aisha replied. "I'm sure."

The deli man gave her the once-over. Aisha could

feel herself tensing up. She took another gulp of coffee and felt the hot liquid enter her bloodstream. She was ready for whatever he was going to tell her. After all, Aisha knew that Carina had been—and probably still was—a drug addict. It wasn't as though Deli Man could tell her anything *shocking*.

"Nice lady," the man mumbled. "But really a shame, really a shame."

Aisha asked him what he meant. He flashed her an odd look. "Run into a bit of trouble is all I'll say," the deli man replied. Aisha could guess what he meant by that.

"Wouldn't be so bad," the man continued, "if it weren't for the fact that there was a kid involved. Man, I hate it when there's an innocent kid affected by things like this." He shook his head forlornly.

"Another cup of coffee?" he asked Aisha. "How 'bout it?"

Aisha could barely manage a nod. She was reeling. If Carina Connelly had a child, then who was the father?

One more cup of coffee and she was on the road. Her mission was now even more imperative.

Lara was bumming. Hard.

Nothing was going her way. The batteries in her clock radio had gone dead while she was napping, so she'd woken up later than she'd wanted to. Then—in the shower—right after she'd lathered her body with a thick coat of moisturizing soap and massaged two large handfuls of shampoo into her short-cropped hair, the water pressure died. She had to dunk her head in the kitchen sink to get the shampoo out. (Of course, that meant taking all the dirty dishes out of the sink, which was in itself quite a feat.) Then, when she'd gone to put on the outfit she wanted to wear tonight—a short black velour minidress with black lace trim—she realized that it had shrunk in the wash. The sleeves had shrunk to three-quarter length, and the dress was so short that it was almost too revealing for Lara to wear (which was really saying something). Not to mention that the washing machine had done something weird to the fabric of the dress, which was now all puckered.

Lara sighed. It looked like it was going to be a jeans and T-shirt kind of evening. Not that anyone in attendance at Zoey Passmore's barbecue deserved much more than that.

Still, Lara liked to look good. Going out in an extra-short skirt and a tiny top always gave her a surge of confidence. And she could use one tonight.

Her luck was going to have to change if she was going to break up Zoey and Lucas. It just had to.

Nina stood over the grill. The scent of burning shrimp wafted upward.

"Nina," Zoey scolded, "those are supposed to be blackened, not burnt! Remember?"

Nina wasn't sure she knew the difference. "Sorry," she mumbled. Well, it was no surprise that she was messing up. As everyone already knew: Domesticity was not her strong suit.

Zoey, on the other hand, was a culinary wonder. Nina watched in amazement as her best friend brushed Cajun spices onto grilled chicken, periodically leaving her post to turn over the crab fritters that were frying in a pan in the kitchen. She was a virtual Betty Crocker.

"You could have your own cooking show, Zo," Nina mused.

"And toss journalism to the wind?" Zoey asked. She

144

was brushing a chicken breast with a dark brown sauce.

"Well, our generation already has Tabitha Soren," Nina replied. "What we really need is a new Martha Stewart. Think about it, Zo. First a cooking show, then a magazine, then a series of books on how to entertain. You'll be a hero to your generation! You can create a lifestyle."

"You've lost it." Zoey laughed. "And anyway, I think our generation already has a lifestyle." She paused.

"What's that?" Nina asked.

"Uh, slacking, Nina," Zoey teased. "Are you familiar with the term?"

"Oh, *that* lifestyle . . ." Nina chuckled. "That's one lifestyle I've cornered the market on."

"Well, I don't know. You're not doing a very good job today—you came out of the house." Zoey smiled. "I'll be right back," she said. "I think I hear the door. The drinks delivery is probably here."

Nina was alone.

On the way over to Zoey's house, Nina had vowed to herself to be as good to Zoey as possible. She'd been really upset about the argument Zoey and she had had yesterday. *It's all my fault,* she'd thought guiltily. *Lucas is being weird to Zoey because of me, and I'm giving Zoey weird advice because I know that Lucas is being weird to her because of me. And she has every right to think that I'm being a jerk because I am. I mean, how could I have put myself in this position? How, how, how?*

Nina was silently berating herself and wishing that the barbecue could just be over already when she felt that she was no longer alone. Somebody had joined her outside, and she didn't need to look up from the blackened shrimp to know who it was.

She felt who it was. In every bone in her body.

"Hey, Lucas." She was trying to keep her voice and demeanor as happy and buoyant as possible. "Pretty is as pretty does," she could hear her stepmother saying. The woman was the master of the greeting-card-style cliché.

"Hey, Nina," Lucas replied. His voice was steady and filled her with unexpected warmth.

If you look at him, you'll break, Nina instructed herself. *If you look him in the eye, you'll want to cry. And if you start crying, you'll want him to hold you. And if he holds you, you'll want him to kiss you. . . .*

Just then Zoey returned. "Look what I brought you, Nina!" She giggled, motioning to Lucas. Nina felt her stomach turn. "A helper!" Zoey answered herself. Nina tried to muster a smile. "Hey," Zoey continued, "I've got to go with my mom to pick out the corn. Can you guys hold down the fort?"

"Sure, Zo," Lucas answered. "No problem."

"Thanks, guys," Zoey chirped. Nina watched out of the corner of her eye as Zoey went to give Lucas a kiss. The sight of Lucas's hand resting comfortably on Zoey's waist sent a chill down her spine.

Zoey blew Nina a kiss. She was gone.

"The trick is to blacken, not burn," Nina mumbled to no one in particular. "Not that I'm entirely sure what that means." Her eyes were peeled to the grilling shrimp.

"You know, you can look at me," Lucas said finally. "Or am I that horrible to look at?"

Nina couldn't bring herself to look up.

"Come on, Nina, you can do it," Lucas teased, a note of sadness in his voice. "I mean, we've got a long day ahead of us. We might as well make the best of it."

"I've been dreading this barbecue from hell." Nina finally faced him. "I mean, you have no idea. . . ."

146

"Oh, I think I do." Lucas laughed. "You think this is how I want to spend my one day off? Grilling the shellfish—which I'm usually catching?"

"Good point," Nina remarked. "Why couldn't Zoey have been more considerate and had frozen fish sticks?"

"Or just cold cereal," Lucas responded. "Why go for fish at all? Why not just have a few boxes of different-flavored cereal?"

"Froot Loops are kinda hard to barbecue," Nina countered. "I learned that in my home ec class."

Lucas chuckled. At the sound of his throaty laugh Nina's eyes finally snapped into focus, and she was able to take in what Lucas looked like.

She sighed at how handsome he was. Zoey had outfitted Lucas in a cooking apron and chef's hat. On most people it would have looked comical and stupid (especially considering the fact that the apron said World's Best Mom), but somehow Lucas made it look manly. The cotton was too tight around his broad chest, and the strings were barely wide enough to encircle his muscular back. Even the hat—haphazardly positioned on Lucas's blond head—looked cute.

"Oh, God, I've gotta get over this." Nina hadn't meant to say that out loud; it just came out. Thank God for the grill, which at that moment let out a sizzling sound.

"What'd you say?" Lucas asked.

"Nothing!" Nina replied brusquely. The grill was spitting out little wafts of smoke, which Nina tried to fan with her arms.

Lucas rescued her by grabbing the skewers from her hand and removing the charred bits of shellfish from the fire.

It was too late.

Nina couldn't tell if it was the heat from the grill or Lucas that she felt so intensely. She felt dizzy.

"Nin," he said softly. "We should probably talk." Nina was seized with the fear that Lucas could read her mind.

"Oh?" Nina asked.

"I miss you," he said. She peered up at him. What could he mean by that? "I mean," he corrected himself, "I miss our friendship. I feel like I haven't talked to you for months. I know it's only been days, but it feels like it's been a long time."

"It feels like a millennium," Nina said softly.

"I hope you understand," Lucas offered. "I care too much about Zoey to mess up her and my relationship. I want to be friends with you, if you think we still can."

Nina felt the heat from the grill rising. She tried to summon up a response. *But what if I've really fallen for you?* she wanted to say.

But saying that would be a huge admittance, and something kept her from making it: Zoey.

As if she'd been channeled via ESP, Zoey returned at that very moment. Her arms were full of brown paper bags, which were overflowing with corn on the cob. "Hey, you guys!" she said. "How's it going?"

"Great!" Lucas offered, rushing over to help her.

"Nin, how'd you do with the shrimp?" Zoey asked, turning to her.

"Okay," Nina replied. "I think they're all dead now."

"Hey, Nin, you're not crying, are you?" Zoey whispered to her friend. "Your eyes look a little puffy."

"It's just the steam from the grill," Nina answered. "Don't worry about me."

Zoey flashed her a look of concern, and Nina mustered a smile. "Whatever you say," Zoey said.

Zoey

What's up with my
brother? He's always got a
secret. The thing is that
this time I feel like he's
having a hard time keeping
it. He hasn't been surfing
in the mornings, and he's
been staying in bed a lot.
I want to ask him if he's
feeling okay, but I feel like
when I ask him anything
like that, he immediately goes
into attack mode. I have a
feeling this is eye related.
Like maybe things are
blurrier than he's letting
on. It's little things I
notice. Like today I saw
him wearing two different
colored socks. And he's
been sitting awfully close
to the television. And the
other day I heard him say
he thought that Lara's pic-

ture was beautifully
painted.
   He's definitely having
trouble seeing.

BENJAMIN

What's up with my sister? I don't
understand what her deal is with
Lara. I know girls can be petty, but
this is ridiculous. Yeah, Lara can be a
little crazy. Yeah, she can be a little
off. But Zoey should recognize that she
is an artist. Artists can be a little tem-
peramental, a little fiery. Zoey's so sta-
ble. But she can't expect everyone else
to be.

Seventeen

"Tell me why I'm going to this barbecue again?" Claire asked Benjamin as they walked along Camden Street.

"Because, Claire," Benjamin explained, "it'll be good for you to get out. You can't just hide in your house all day."

"Why?" Claire asked. "It's a lot safer that way. I mean, who knows where *he'll* be next?"

"Well, if he's following us, I'll see him." The words hung on Benjamin's lips. He'd said them so confidently, but he knew they were only half true. He'd been at the doctor's today. "Everything's gonna be a bit blurry for a while, Ben," he'd said. "Unless you take it easy and do your exercises."

"I'm telling you, Benjamin," Claire said. "I feel like he's behind us right now. I feel like he's following me all the time."

Benjamin swung around. There was a crowd of kids behind them, a couple of girls jumping rope and walking simultaneously, an old couple holding hands, a couple of fishermen, and some skinny computer-nerd-looking type of guy.

No one who looked like they had stalker potential.

* * *

Sean kept ten steps back.

What does she see in that guy? he wondered angrily. *He's not so great looking. I bet she treats him really badly. Some guys are such suckers.*

Sean sucked noisily on a watermelon Jolly Rancher. Just the sight of that girl—her long black hair, her long legs, her confident smile—filled him with a million different emotions.

Sean watched as the guy scanned the crowds. He was squinting hard, then he turned back around, and he and Claire resumed their pace.

They don't know I'm here. Sean chuckled merrily to himself.

For the first time in his life, feeling invisible felt empowering.

Claire wouldn't let Benjamin leave her side. "Please, Benjamin, just sit here with me. I can't deal with anyone else today."

"I just want to get some food before it gets cold," Benjamin protested.

He and Claire were sitting apart from everyone else in a corner of the Passmores' family room. Benjamin had to admit: He was glad to have a reason not to mill around. Watching Nina barbecue shrimp was a little more than he could handle. The two of them had exchanged a terse hello, but Benjamin couldn't help feeling that Nina was barely aware of the awkwardness between them. Apparently she had other things on her mind.

Benjamin settled for a bag of chips that was on the table. He sat back down next to Claire.

"Benjamin," she whispered. "I'm all for taking matters into our own hands, but before we do, are you sure we shouldn't reconsider going to the police?"

"There's nothing the police can do," Benjamin said. "I wish it were otherwise, but they can't do anything unless you have concrete evidence that somebody intends to hurt you. Now it just looks like some random practical joker is after you."

Claire shook her head. "I guess," she said. "I mean, I'm sure they have better things to do than be on the lookout for some phantom stalker. But still, you'd think a dead mouse and a destroyed wardrobe would fall somewhere within the boundaries of disturbing the peace!"

"Claire, I promise we'll take care of it," Benjamin replied steadily. "I'm going to help you catch him." He felt like a superhero character in a comic book, soothing the damsel in distress.

"I wish I knew how to defend myself," Claire muttered mournfully. "I think I should take martial arts or something. Tae kwon do, maybe. Did I tell you what happened with my computer?" she continued. "It totally froze up on me while I was midsentence. It was really weird."

"Maybe it's a virus?" Ben asked.

"I don't think so," Claire said. "I'd just run an antiviral program. It's something else."

Does Claire think the stalker's a hacker? Benjamin wondered. He was about to ask her just that when Zoey walked by. "Benjamin, there you are," she said.

"Hey, Zo," Benjamin replied.

"Benjamin," Zoey said. "I don't mean to be a pain, but do you think you could help me out and mingle? I mean, it's weird that you guys are just sitting here."

Benjamin nodded okay, but he knew he just couldn't do it. Neither he nor Claire really felt up to socializing. They had too much on their minds.

Sean could smell the sweet scents of corn on the cob cooking on the grill and spicy chicken breasts sizzling.

She better not be in there all night, he grumbled. *I'm going to get hungry soon.*

Sean hadn't had an easy time situating himself outside the Passmores' house. There weren't that many places for him to hide. Finally he'd crouched behind some hedges.

This is what you get for dumping me, Sean grumbled menacingly to himself. *This is what you get for using and abusing people,* he added. *I was nothing but type-face to you, Claire Geiger. Well, I'm a whole lot more now, aren't I?*

Sean removed the Polaroid picture he'd taken of Claire today. *If only you weren't so pretty,* he thought. *If only you weren't so perfect looking.*

Sean felt his fingers start to twitch, and the picture shook in his hand. *Our communication meant nothing to you, Weather Girl, did it?*

Sean took a Sharpie pen from his pocket and scrawled all over the face in the picture. In the photo Claire looked shocked.

But not as shocked as you'll be tonight, Weather Girl, Sean thought angrily. *When you receive another package for Ms. Claire Geiger.*

He placed the Polaroid in the off-white envelope and sealed it.

"Look, Claire," Benjamin whispered, "I think we've got a foolproof plan."

"Foolproof," Claire agreed. "But is it psycho-proof?"

Benjamin suppressed a laugh. "Uh, I should think so," he mumbled.

"So tonight?" Claire asked. "We get him tonight?"

"Yes," Benjamin said confidently. "Tonight, Claire, your nightmare will be over."

Eighteen

Aisha sat on the puce-colored sofa, surveying the unfamiliar living room. The room smelled sweet and sour at once—like a mixture of condensed milk, baby vomit, old food (there was an empty pizza box on the table and an open carton of hot and sour soup lying on the floor), and cheap room deodorizer.

"So you're not a social worker?" Carina called out from the bedroom.

"N-N-No," Aisha stammered. "I'm very sure."

After her meeting with the deli man Aisha had gotten up the motivation to go and knock on Carina's door. After all, if Carina had a baby, then it was possible that Christopher was the father. *Is that his secret?* Aisha wondered. *Is that why he wouldn't tell me about Carina? Because if I found out about her, I'd find out about Carmen?*

Aisha glanced at the playpen on the floor, where Carmen was playing. Carina had introduced her to Carmen when she'd entered the house. She'd let Aisha in the door after a few questions: "Are you selling something? Are you with the welfare committee? Are you from the Child Protection Agency?" Aisha had shaken her head no to all the questions. "Oh, well, then have a seat," Carina had said, ushering Aisha to a clean spot on the sofa. "I need to go and take care of a few things in the bedroom, but why don't you get to know Carmen." Carina had disappeared, leaving Aisha alone with her child.

Aisha was kind of relieved. This gave her the chance to do a little prep work. She took her notebook out of her bag and opened it to her list of questions, although looking over them, she realized she now had a lot more, the leadoff being: "Is Christopher Shupe the father of your baby?"

Aisha studied baby Carmen for traces of Shupe lineage, but it was hard to tell. She certainly was a beautiful baby—with tiny little corkscrew curls around her wide face, plush pink lips that suckled a pacifier, soft brown skin that was perhaps a bit more olive toned than either Carina's or Christopher's. "Hey, baby," Aisha murmured sweetly, sticking out her hand to the toddler. Carmen latched onto her finger. Her little hand felt wet and clammy as it clutched Aisha's.

"Mommy?" Carmen said.

"Mommy will be right out," she whispered.

"Ring," Carmen said, moving her little fingers' grasp to Aisha's ring finger.

"Yes," Aisha answered. "Very good. That's a ring."

"Mommy's ring," the baby said inexplicably.

"No," Aisha said. "My ring." Carmen just gurgled.

Aisha had a sudden burst of panic. What if this ring had once belonged to Carina? What if it was a second-hand ring? Then Carmen would be right. Indeed it would have been "Mommy's ring."

To Aisha, Carmen looked about two years old. If Christopher was the father, the timing would make sense. "Oh, my God," Aisha murmured. "I bet it is true. It is him." What kind of person would abandon his child? Who was this man she was supposed to marry?

Aisha's brain was working overtime. She started tabulating figures and dates in her head, trying to figure out how pregnant Carina could have been when Christopher left her, how old Carmen would have been when Christopher moved to Chatham. . . .

Her head was spinning as Carina reentered the room. Aisha was surprised by what she saw. When Carina had answered the door, she'd been wearing a bathrobe with her hair up turban style in a pink-and-white-flowered towel that was fraying on the ends. Now her wet hair hung in loose curls around her face, and she wore a blue-and-white polka-dotted dress that came down to her calves. It was short sleeved, and Aisha could see how skinny Carina really was. There didn't seem to be an ounce of fat on her. Even her face seemed gaunt, and there were dark circles under her eyes.

"So tell me," Carina said. "How can I help you?"

Aisha began to talk. She didn't need her notebook to guide her. It just all spilled out.

"Let me get this straight," Zoey said quietly. "Benjamin spent the entire barbecue glued to Claire, and after he walks Claire home, he has the nerve to bring *her.* Do you think," she asked Lucas, "that he has a drug problem?"

Lucas shrugged. "Can't tell ya, Zo," he replied.

By *her,* Zoey meant Lara, and she was none too pleased to see that Lara was enjoying the last of the leftovers. "I wanted to keep those for lunch tomorrow," Zoey grumbled.

"Oh, Zo, maybe it's time you just forgot about her," Lucas said.

"Forget about her!" Zoey groaned. "How could I? I mean, she's always here. The girl's like mold that keeps reappearing."

"Well, she is your sister," Lucas mentioned, shrugging.

"Half sister," Zoey corrected, "emphasis on the half. And doesn't it seem like she keeps looking at us weirdly, Lucas? Don't you get the feeling that she's watching us?"

"No," Lucas countered. "I'm sorry, Zo, I don't."

"She is," Zoey complained. "I know she is."

Zoey was pretty annoyed to see Lara, but otherwise she was pleased. The barbecue had been a decent success, and she and Lucas were getting along well. In fact, Lucas had been attentive all night—helping her husk the corn, change the charcoal, light the fires, disassemble the grills. And she'd even seen him and Nina exchange a couple of words.

"Look, Lucas," Zoey mumbled, pinching him and directing his gaze toward Lara. "She's staring straight at us."

"Maybe it's because you're so pretty, and she's jealous," Lucas teased, giving Zoey's hair a quick pull.

"Or maybe it's because she's crazy," Zoey quipped.

"Christopher's ashamed of me," Carina gasped. Her head was in her hands, and her skinny body was shaking with muffled sobs.

Aisha didn't know what she'd expected to happen, but reducing Carina to tears was not among them. But here the poor woman was—a sobbing, sniffling disaster. *Oh, my God,* Aisha thought. *What have I done?*

"He shouldn't be," Aisha said firmly. Carina's tears had put Aisha on her side. "He has no right to be!" *It should be the other way around,* Aisha thought angrily. She hadn't come out and asked directly whether Carmen was Christopher's baby, but from the details Carina had given her—she and Christopher had been desperately in love; they'd gotten married because

Christopher wanted to save her from a bad family situation; they'd had it annulled because she'd had a "little problem," one she didn't have now; she'd tried to stay in touch with Christopher since they had so much in common still, such an important past together (from that Aisha inferred that Carina meant Carmen)—she'd assumed that Christopher was indeed the father.

"He should marry you," Carina said humbly between sobs. She looked up at Aisha, who stared straight back into her red-rimmed, sunken eyes. "You're pretty." Carina's mouth twisted. "And you seem very smart."

"Thank you," Aisha said. She didn't know what else to say.

"And don't take this the wrong way," Carina offered. "But you remind me of all the things I used to be. Before everything . . ."

Aisha didn't know what Carina meant by "everything." *You mean before Christopher Shupe ruined your life?* she wanted to ask. But for some reason she held back.

"It was really nice being with you tonight, Lucas." Zoey sighed, gently caressing the back of his neck as she hugged him good-bye. She knew she was supposed to keep it light, that she wasn't supposed to mention anything serious, but she couldn't help adding: "And I'm really sorry about that fight we had on the docks. I don't want you to think that I think anything but good things about you."

Lucas kissed her on the top of the forehead. "It's okay, Zo," he said. "I know you didn't mean anything. I just get in a bad mood when I'm on the boat all the time. I'm sorry if I took it out on you."

"Please, let's spend more time together," Zoey pleaded. "I mean, Lucas, just think about it . . . I don't have much time left to be with you."

Lucas didn't say anything. He just hugged Zoey harder. "Let's finish cleaning up, Zo," he said. "I gotta get going soon. Boat tomorrow, you know."

Zoey nodded. The rift was gone . . . again. Lucas was back to normal.

But why was Lara staring at them?

Aisha was convinced. Christopher Shupe was a total liar. A deceitful, horrible, neglectful guy who'd ditched this troubled girl and this beautiful baby.

She was putting her notebook back in her bag. "Are you sure you don't want to stay for dinner?" Carina was asking. "I could order pizza."

In the half hour that she'd been there, Aisha had noticed that the place had begun to smell worse and worse. Carmen's diapers needed changing, the garbage was rotting. . . . The thought of eating there filled her with a horrific sense of dread.

Maybe she should take Carina and Carmen out for dinner. It wasn't beyond her means, considering that her parents had given her some spending money to take to Princeton. She was about to suggest it when the doorbell rang.

"One sec," Carina said. Aisha watched as Carina walked to the front door. Her body looked even skinnier from behind. The sun coming in from the front window made her dress slightly translucent, and her body looked practically skeletal.

Carina talked to the person at the door, but she didn't let whoever it was in. "I have company," Aisha heard her say. "I'm busy now." Then, "No, Carmen does not want to see you."

From the angle where she was sitting, all Aisha could see was a shadowy figure, although she was pretty certain it'd been a male voice that she'd heard.

"Baby formula," Carina said when she walked back

161

in the room, holding up a small brown paper bag. "My friend," she muttered. "I needed him to go and pick it up for me."

"I could have gotten it for you," Aisha said.

Aisha was about to mention the dinner thing when Carmen started crying. "Well, I guess you got the formula just in time," Aisha mentioned.

"I guess so," Carina agreed. She crossed the room to the playpen, still clutching the paper bag.

"Is there anything I can do?" Aisha offered. Carmen was practically wailing now, and Aisha had to scream to be heard.

"No, that's okay," Carina screamed back. "I'm just going to take her in the bedroom for a sec. Change her."

As Carina lifted the baby from her playpen Carmen started to cry even harder. It was as if she were sobbing in stereo. (Not one for many tears herself, Aisha realized she probably had heard more crying today than she had in the past year.) Then the baby started to kick Carina with her little feet. She was a big baby, and Carina was a small woman, and Aisha watched in horror as Carina almost lost her grip on the child.

But Carina managed to keep Carmen in her arms. What she did lose was the brown paper bag, which tumbled to the floor.

"I'll get that," Carina practically shouted, trying to manage the squirming baby and pick up the bag. But Carmen gave her a kick in the chest. Aisha crossed the room to help. When she went to pick up the bag, she realized its contents had spilled out.

There was no baby formula there; only a bag of black tarlike substance and a dark wooden pipe.

The baby kept crying.

Nineteen

What were Lucas and Zoey whispering to each other about? Lara had to know. She tried her hardest to get as close to the kitchen as possible, but each time she made a move toward the kitchen, someone in the Passmore clan derailed her. "Lara, can you come over here? I want to show you this picture in an art book," her father said, pointing to a old oil painting of a Renaissance king. "Do you think you can make my portrait look like that?"

"Hey, Lara, I've been talking to Dad about the schedule for our pasta cooking classes," Benjamin cried, motioning to her to come and look at a piece of paper in his hand. "Look, an entire hour devoted to pesto! How about that?"

"Lara, do you think you could help me take out the garbage?" Mrs. Passmore had asked. "Just grab that bag of corn husks, will you?"

With all the Passmores on her back, Lara had barely had a moment to do what she'd come to the barbecue to do: keep tabs on Zoey and Lucas. Mainly Lucas. She needed to follow up on her suspicion that he was hiding something from Zoey. Lara had a special knack for smelling out secrets, and she had a supreme sense that Lucas had one.

But one wouldn't know from watching Zoey and Lucas in action. They were giggling and tittering and whispering to each other like annoying little lovebirds.

"Lucas, will you help me take the tablecloths down to the laundry room?" Lara heard Zoey chirp.

"Sure thing, Zo," she heard Lucas respond.

She decided to seize the opportunity and ran to bump heads with the couple as they were coming out of the kitchen doorway. "You guys need any help?" she asked.

She watched Zoey and Lucas exchange a suspicious glance. *They act like I'm dangerous,* she thought, annoyed.

"Uh, that's okay," Zoey replied saucily. "We wouldn't want you to put yourself out."

"No problem," Lara demurred, ignoring Zoey's snootiness. She wasn't going to let her prissy little half sister get to her tonight. After all, she was on a mission.

"Uh, we've got it," Lucas stumbled, grabbing his girlfriend by the elbow and flashing Lara a weak and oh-so-phony smile. The two of them walked away, leaving her standing there alone.

He hadn't said anything to prove her suspicions, but there was something about the way that Lucas was clinging to Zoey. It was so different from when she'd seen them on the docks. Nobody could go from cold to hot that fast. Unless they were confused. Or pretending to feel something they weren't.

Lara knew in her heart that Lucas was hiding something. A master of deception herself, she could sense it in others from a mile away.

Nina bit her bottom lip. It was chapped and crackly and dry, and it still tasted like barbecue sauce. She thought about searching the bottom of her backpack for the banana berry lip balm she generally kept close by, but she stopped herself. For some reason, right now, Nina liked the pain.

Nina had decided to take the long way home along the docks for a couple of reasons. Mainly because she'd wanted to avoid running into Benjamin and Claire, who'd taken the regular route home. She had no idea why the two of them were hanging out so much, but she definitely didn't want any part of it. There was a dark part of her heart that whispered they might be getting back together, but Nina didn't really believe that. They weren't acting like they were in love—they were acting creepy and secretive. Between the weird exchange of whispers and phone calls and Claire's brand-new outfits, you'd think the two were spies or something. Maybe Claire was working on a new identity. *Anything would be better than the one she's got now,* Nina thought.

The other reason that Nina had taken the long route home was that she'd needed time to think. A lot had happened at the barbecue. She and Lucas had spent some time together alone. They hadn't said anything that substantive, but they'd definitely come to an agreement: Nothing was ever going to happen between them. It was all for the best. Really, it was.

Nina bit her lip. The blood she drew tasted salty—like sea air.

Lara sat on the Passmores' living-room couch, pretending to read her father's art book and watching from the corner of her eye as Zoey and Lucas said their good-byes.

When Lucas had been gone two minutes, she decided to slink out of the house after him. She didn't say good-bye to anyone. There wasn't time.

Twenty

Lucas didn't know why, but for some reason the minute he walked outside the Passmore house, he was awake. Wide awake. He knew he should go straight home to bed. After all, he had a work shift in a matter of hours. But something inspired him to take a walk.

Lucas finally felt that things were straight between him and Zoey. He'd cleared up stuff with Nina, put the kissing fiasco behind him. Maybe they could even be friends in a normal way now.

Lucas felt the sea breeze whip against the side of his neck as he walked along the docks. The sun was down now, and the only lights came from the lighthouse off in the distance.

Lucas liked being out at this time of night. There was no one around. It'd be a few hours until the grizzled old fishermen hit the boats and their incessant complaining filled the air. For now it was quiet, and Lucas was temporarily at peace.

Lucas put his hands in the pockets of his hooded sweatshirt and continued the walk toward the lighthouse. Once he got there, he'd turn around and come back. He thought for a second he heard something behind him, but when he whipped his head around, no one was there. *Probably an animal or something,* he told himself.

It was when Lucas was about halfway there that he spotted a figure in the distance. It was a small figure, and it was shuffling slowly toward him, although it didn't look up to see him.

Lucas could tell who it was from the sad swagger and downturned gaze. It was Nina Geiger. He thought about turning around, but he felt compelled to make sure she was okay.

After all, that's what friends did for each other.

Benjamin knew he was right. The stalker was going to show up tonight. After all, according to everything Claire had told him, he showed up every night, so it wasn't really such a brilliant deduction.

Benjamin had walked Claire home, then returned to the party. He and Claire figured that if the madman was following them, he'd see Benjamin leave and figure he wasn't coming back. "That'll probably make him overconfident," Benjamin had told Claire. Then Benjamin could come back and sneak behind the hedges in front of the house. He'd read a couple of magazine articles about stalkers that he'd gotten off the Internet, and he'd read that the stalker profile was obsessive, compulsive, and usually incredibly narcissistic—they thought they were smarter than everybody else. Not that he couldn't have figured that out without the article.

"Do you see anything?" Claire hissed from the kitchen window.

"Shhh, Claire," Benjamin scolded her. "Keep it down. If he's coming, you know he's going to probably be really silent about it. He's probably a professional."

"What do you mean, a professional?" Claire hissed back. "You think you can go to summer camp for this or something?"

Benjamin was about to compose an answer when he

saw a shadowy figure coming toward the house. He squinted in an attempt to adjust his vision to the darkness. "Duck," he hissed to Claire.

Benjamin watched as the figure approached. Benjamin couldn't see much, but he could tell that the shadow was that of a tall and lean man. The guy was so close to Benjamin, he could hear him breathing. "Here you go, Weather Girl," the guy mumbled cryptically.

Weather Girl? Benjamin thought. *Who's Weather Girl?*

The guy dropped off an envelope, and before Benjamin knew it, he'd evaporated. "This dude's faster than I thought," Benjamin muttered, scrambling to get to his feet. The plan had been to run after the guy and corner him, and now it was almost too late.

Benjamin squinted into the night.

He thought he saw the shadow lurking on the front walkway and he ran toward it, but it was just the shade cast by the Geigers' oak tree. He ran forward into the darkness, listening for footsteps, but there were none.

He'd failed. Or rather: His eyesight had failed him.

Benjamin walked somberly back to the house. He picked up the envelope on the way in. It felt like there was something inside it, a photograph or something.

"What happened?" Claire begged when she saw him. He looked at her forlornly.

"Claire," he moaned, "I missed him. I should have gotten him, though."

"Should have?" Claire asked. "What do you mean, should have? Did you see him? What did he look like?"

"Claire," Benjamin intoned. "I didn't see anything."

"Excuse me?" she said. "You were right next to him!"

"Yeah," Benjamin said. "But I didn't see anything."

He had a lot of explaining to do.

* * *

Before Lucas knew what happened, he was face-to-face with Nina Geiger. "What's going on, Nin?" he asked.

"Not much," she replied. "Just walking, I guess."

"Like you were 'just walking' the other night?" Lucas asked. He was referring to the last time they'd run into each other, the night they'd almost kissed, had both wanted to, but didn't.

"I guess," Nina said, peering up at him with her big gray eyes. They were wet with tears.

"Oh, Nina!" Lucas said softly, touching a tear with his fingertip. "What's wrong?"

Nina sucked in her breath, and before she could say "Nothing," Lucas had his arms around her. His embrace engulfed her. Nina pressed her tiny round face into his chest.

"I'm getting your sweatshirt all wet," she said.

"It's okay," Lucas said, rubbing her back. "It's all right. Everything's going to be all right."

Nina didn't want to feel this way.

But she *needed* to. She needed to feel that someone cared for her. But why did it have to be Lucas?

"Don't worry, Nina," Lucas said, and she felt the rumbling of his chest as he spoke. The vibrations sent a warm shiver through her body. She raised her face to look into Lucas's eyes, and before she knew what she was doing, she took his face in her hands and kissed him.

Lara couldn't believe her luck. This week was finally turning around. So this was Lucas's secret. She smiled to herself—this was good. Very, very good. Or very bad—for Lucas.

Lara had seen it all.

He was having a relationship with someone other than Zoey; someone none other than Zoey's best friend.

It was more than she could ever have asked for.

Making Out:
Now Zoey's Alone

Book 24 in the explosive series about broken hearts, secrets, friendship, and of course, love.

Lara saw **Lucas** kiss **Nina** and now she has power over **Zoey**. With **Lara, Nina,** and **Lucas** sharing guilty secrets, **Zoey** feels left out in the cold. Can she trust the people she loves the most? The truth will be hard to find...

MAKING OUT

by KATHERINE APPLEGATE

(#14) Aaron lets go	80870-6/$3.99 US/$5.50 Can
(#15) Who loves Kate?	80871-4/$3.99 US/$5.50 Can
(#16) Lara gets even	80872-2/$3.99 US/$5.50 Can
(#17) Two-timing Aisha	81119-7/$3.99 US/$5.50 Can
(#18) Zoey speaks out	81120-0/$3.99 US/$5.99 Can
(#19) Kate finds love	81121-9/$3.99 US/$5.99 Can
(#20) Never trust Lara	81309-2/$3.99 US/$5.99 Can
(#21) Trouble with Aaron	81310-6/$3.99 US/$5.95 Can
(#22) Always loving Zoey	81311-4/$3.99 US/$5.95 Can
(#23) Lara gets lucky	81527-3/$3.99 US/$5.95 Can